JUST
MARRIED

BOOKS BY KIERSTEN MODGLIN

JUST MARRIED

KIERSTEN MODGLIN

bookouture

Published by Bookouture in 2021

An imprint of Storyfire Ltd.
Carmelite House
50 Victoria Embankment
London EC4Y 0DZ

www.bookouture.com

ISBN: 978-1-80019-637-7
eBook ISBN: 978-1-80019-636-0

To my husband, for never minding too much when I turn our beautiful vacations into stories you can't read in the dark.

EPIGRAPH

"The shadows are as important as the light."
—Charlotte Brontë

PROLOGUE

Death has a smell—strange and ineffable. Primal. Like birth. Like the smell of the baby when it was born. Like the smell of a room filled with grief, of tears, of hopelessness. Somehow, as I stared up into the windows of the house that night, at the glowing amber beams from beyond the glass, I knew I would smell it again.

I knew what was coming before it did.

I can't explain it. It doesn't make any sense, even now, how I knew. But there it was. A niggle in my brain.

She's going to die.

He's going to kill her.

I was going to smell death again.

I watched in absolute, chilling horror as he led her up the staircase toward the second floor. It was where it would happen. Somehow, I knew. It was where it had happened before.

I should've moved, should've done something. But what was there to do? I watched him take her hand, sliding it up over her arm. She stumbled. Had she been drinking? It wasn't unlikely. When he spun her around, his back to the window, I saw the blade. Even from where I was, hidden in the vast darkness of the forest, it was there.

Once he pulled it from his belt, it was over. I had no chance of saving her then. I moved forward, out of the safety of the trees and shadows, pushing myself to move faster despite my legs begging me to slow down. My joints ached, my ankle throbbing from a recent sprain, and I knew the wound on my side had ripped open.

It hadn't healed well anyway. I'd only cleaned it with water, using bits of a shirt I'd torn up to tie around my waist until it stopped bleeding. I needed to see a doctor, but that didn't matter. I never would. It would heal on its own or I would die, like every other wound I'd ever suffered.

Forgetting my own pain, I glanced back up at the window, where the blade had been pulled out.

I was too late.

He held it above her, more for show than anything. She didn't move—frozen in fear. I didn't either. Couldn't.

My breath caught in my chest as I tried to decide what to do. What could I do? She didn't move as he lowered the blade to her chest, but I heard her scream. It cut through the glass, through the silence of the forest, sending chills across my goosebump-lined arms.

He lifted the blade again, bringing it to her stomach as she fell backward with a solid swipe. With this blow, she crumpled, and the horror in my chest exploded, cold spreading to every part of my extremities.

She was dead.

He dropped the knife, taking a half-step back and looking over what he had done. I watched as his hand raised to rub across his lips, and he shook his head. His foot lifted from the ground, and he kicked her hip forcefully. When she didn't move, he bent down. For just a moment, I thought he was going to attend to her.

Instead, he picked up the knife, swiped it off on his shirt, and slid it back into his belt. When he stood, he kicked her again, and my stomach rumbled. I was going to be sick, but I hadn't eaten much in days. What could I possibly still be retaining that I could expel?

When I looked up, the man was gone from the window, though her body still lay there on the floor. I almost rolled my eyes at the thought—*where else would it go?*

Then, panic jolted through me as I looked back up to where he'd been standing. Could he see me from where I was? In the light from the porch, it was possible. I was no longer hidden.

Could he be coming for me next?

I didn't have time to think.

I had to act.

And so, I ran.

PART ONE

CHAPTER ONE

Ryan

"You know what I've been thinking?" Her feet were resting in my lap, the dark purple polish on her pinkie toe chipped slightly, and her head was leaned back on the chain of the porch swing, a mug of steaming tea resting on her stomach.

She opened her eyes. "What's that?"

"I was thinking we should finally take our honeymoon."

The wrinkle in her forehead deepened as she stared at me. "What are you talking about? I thought we'd agreed to wait awhile." She sat up in the swing, tucking a foot up under her.

I smiled, resting a hand on her knee. "Well, we did. But that was because work was so busy for me and you were still getting settled into the house, but you're all moved in now and I hit my quarterly goal ahead of schedule. I could take the time off and still hit payout this month, no problem. Besides, I'd like some alone time with my wife."

She lifted the mug to her lips without speaking. She was always doing that, making me wait for her to respond, drawing out the silence. Most women I knew talked incessantly, about anything and everything on their mind. Grace was different. She was a thinker, someone who contemplated every word that came from her mouth. She knew that I hung on every word, waiting anxiously for when she'd let me see what that beautiful mind was thinking of next.

"Where were you thinking of going?"

"I hadn't decided just yet. I wanted to see if you were open to it first. I know we said we'd wait and save for the year, but…" I laughed under my breath. "Well, changing my mind isn't a crime, is it?"

She switched the hand that her tea was in and used her free hand to pat my cheek. I could smell her warm, honey scent as soon as her skin drew near me. "It's definitely not a crime." She wrinkled her nose at me. "I think it could be good for us. To get away, clear our heads… just the two of us… It sounds really nice. Where were you thinking of going?"

"Well, I don't have any concrete ideas yet. I know you've always wanted to go to Maine in the fall, so that would be an option. Or Colorado, for the mountains. Somewhere secluded, quiet. Somewhere we can just be together and not worry about anything else."

The smile was slow to spread to her lips, but finally, I saw it. "Well, you've sold me."

"Yeah?" I asked.

"Yeah." She giggled. "If it means I get my husband all to myself and don't have to discuss mortgage rates or pre-approvals or anything else job-related for any length of time, I'm in."

I moved her hand from my cheek, kissing her fingertips. "Deal. Do you think you can get the time off work soon?"

"I'll talk to Janet, but I can't see why not. The bookshop's been slow lately, and I'm sure she and Isaac can handle it for a week as long as I give her enough notice."

"Well, let me get everything in order, and then I'll give you the exact dates to talk to her about, okay?"

"Fine, but don't keep me waiting too long." She took another sip of her tea. "You've gotten me excited now."

"Oh, I have, have I?" I teased, wiggling my eyebrows. She smirked, rolling her eyes and looking away. I cleared my throat, speaking seriously then, "Maybe we can time it with your fertile window. How surprised would everyone be if we came back from our honeymoon pregnant?"

"We'd be a cliché," she said flatly. "And besides, that's not quite how it works. Even if I got pregnant, we wouldn't know for weeks."

"I'm only teasing," I said, rubbing her belly as if there were already a baby—*our* baby—inside. She stiffened under my touch, and I pulled away.

"Anyway, my fertile time is right now, so we would have to wait until next month to go if that's your plan."

"It is?" We hadn't officially been trying, but it had been discussed quite often. I wanted us to start trying for a child right after our wedding. Hell, I would've been happy to have one nine months to the day after. My parents had trouble conceiving; I was their only child, and I saw that struggle firsthand as they tried and failed over and over to have another.

Grace didn't have endometriosis like Mom, I reminded myself, but even still, I didn't want to take any chances. We were much older than my parents had been when they'd been trying, after all. I wanted babies, lots of them, and I wanted them with her.

Grace often said that if a man my age wasn't married or divorced, it typically meant he wasn't ready for that sort of commitment, but I proved her wrong by proposing six months after we'd started dating. We were married two months after that. I'd done all I could to show her how serious I was about her, about our family, and I couldn't wait for the day we'd bring a child into the house I'd bought years ago, even though I was just nineteen, with my future family already in mind.

I looked down at her bare legs, lined with goosebumps from the chilly, fall air. They were lined with sandpaper-like hair. She'd always shaved for me before. Was this a sign that she was getting more comfortable with me? Or that she wasn't interested in having sex with me anymore? I couldn't decide.

"What's wrong?" she asked, studying me.

I ran my hands across her legs. "I thought you'd want to *do it…*"

She twisted her lips into a sly smile. "Who says I don't?"

"Well, you didn't shave. *Not that I care,*" I added quickly. "I've just always known what was on your mind when you came to me all, you know, *silky smooth.*" I laughed awkwardly, my face burning with embarrassment. *Good God, what is wrong with me?*

To my relief, she laughed, loudly and boisterously, then ran her leg against my hands. "If you think I'm going to shave for you all winter, you've got another thing coming, Ryan. You had the unfortunate coincidence of dating me last winter, so I did shave constantly, and then, of course I shaved all summer, because I wore shorts so much. But it's winter now. It's officially sweater, chai tea, and ditch-the-razors season." She laughed again. "You're experiencing me in all of my glory now, and I've got the paperwork that says you're stuck with me regardless."

I ran my hand up her thigh, gripping it seductively. "Oh, I am, am I?" She pressed her lips together, beaming at me.

"Mhm."

"Well, lucky for us both, I wouldn't want it any other way."

"I'm a lucky girl," she whispered, her expression oozing desire as she leaned forward toward me. I cupped her face, pressing my lips to hers again, this time with no intention of breaking apart. She had no idea how wrong she was—*she* wasn't the lucky one. Not even close.

CHAPTER TWO

Grace

Two weeks later

"Are you sure you're going to be okay?" I asked for the hundredth time, patting Stanley's head. He stared back at me with glum, milky eyes. I hated leaving him, but Ryan was so excited. I could hardly tell him no. Besides, without me having to ask, he'd chosen a vacation spot just four hours away, rather than twenty-two or more, like he'd originally talked about. We wouldn't be far from home if something were to happen.

"We'll be fine," Everleigh promised, leaning in for a hug as I stood. "He's going to help Auntie Everleigh lose her last fifteen pounds."

I hugged her back, shaking my head. "Don't subject my best friend to any sort of crazy exercise routine."

"I thought *I* was your best friend." She blinked her eyelashes at me playfully.

"That's what I let you think," I teased. My best friend was perpetually on a diet, and though she managed to take the pounds off occasionally, she always managed to put them back on. I didn't know what she was worried about honestly—despite the weight she hated, or maybe even because of it, she was undeniably beautiful. I would've killed for an ounce of her beauty or personality.

I was on the thin side, but incredibly plain. My nose was large, my lips too small, my eyes too close together. My hair was mousy and frail, rather than long and full, like I would've preferred. No matter how I applied my makeup or styled my hair, I'd never been what most would consider beautiful. At least, until Ryan came along.

Despite my own insecurities about my appearance, I had an amazing man who made me feel like the only woman in the room. It was the one thing Everleigh didn't have... at this moment, at least. That didn't stop her from going out and making the most of her life. Two years younger than me, she was definitely my closest friend, but our differences couldn't be ignored. Besides age and physique, she was wild, while I was calm. She slept around a lot, and I'd only been with two men before Ryan. She'd grown up in a warm, loving family, while both my parents died when I was young.

We were complete opposites, but our grief brought us together. When her older sister, my best friend at the time, died years earlier, Everleigh had needed me as much as I had needed her. The rest, as they say, is history.

"We'll be fine," she repeated, patting his head.

"Just take it easy. And make sure he gets his medicine. It's—"

"*On the counter,*" she finished my sentence for me. "I know. I'll make sure he eats. *Only* healthy treats. He'll get his medicine twice a day. And... what was that last thing? I know I'm forgetting something..."

I tried to think right along with her.

Her eyes lit up. "Oh, yeah, it was something about how I should have lots of wild parties while you're away, right?"

"Don't even joke about that," Ryan warned, appearing behind us, the last of our luggage slung over his back. He kissed my cheek. "Grace will end up backing out on me, and it's too late to get our money refunded."

At our feet, Stanley nuzzled into my knee, and I rubbed his head again. *I'll miss you too, old man.* "Seriously, I can't thank you enough for taking care of him for us." Stanley had gone everywhere with me from the day I got him six years ago, but car rides were too hard on him now. He was an older dog when I'd adopted him, sitting in the back corner of his kennel at the Humane Society I'd worked at in college. I couldn't leave him there to die, so even though I had no space for him in my life and the vet told me he wouldn't make it even five more years most likely, I had to bring him home. My life had revolved around him ever since. Until I met Ryan.

"You know I'll do anything for you guys," Everleigh said, interrupting my thoughts. She rested a hand on my shoulder, frowning slightly as her eyes met mine. "You deserve this, Grace. Take some time off with your hunk of a husband." She winked. Everleigh was one of the only people alive who could still pull off a wink. "And we'll be here when you get back. I promise everything will be fine. I'll take care of your boy as long as Ryan takes care of my girl."

"You know I will," Ryan teased.

I nodded, my fingers already itching to check the list on my phone to be sure we weren't forgetting anything. I'd triple checked the bags after packing them, first crossing everything off the list, then *checking* it off the list, then *X-ing* it out. We had everything, I knew we had everything, but that didn't seem to matter to the ever-present worry in my head.

"Okay, we'll be back on Saturday. You guys have fun, okay?" I patted Stanley's head one last time and stepped away as Ryan put the last of the suitcases and grocery bags into the car and slammed the door.

"We will. Lots of safe, calm fun. You guys don't get too wild out in the mountains, okay?"

"I put some extra cash beside the microwave, Everleigh," Ryan called as he opened his door. "Order yourself some dinner on us."

"You didn't have to do that." Her jaw dropped at the polite gesture, and I couldn't hide my grin. She'd never had great taste in men, so it took very little to surprise or delight her.

"Consider it our thanks," Ryan said casually. "It's the least we could do."

"You sure you don't have any brothers, Ryan?" she asked with a laugh.

He chuckled. "Not that I'm aware of. Call us if you have any trouble, okay?"

"I will, but I won't. I meant what I said, though. You take care of my girl, dude. No snakes or bears or broken bones… you hear me?"

He put two fingers to his forehead and swiped them toward her in a salute. "Scout's honor."

"I am a full-grown, walking, talking adult capable of taking care of herself, you know?" I butted in, rolling my eyes playfully as I opened the door to my side of the car.

"Doesn't stop me from worrying about you," she added, and there was a hint of vulnerability there. She didn't like to be alone, not even for short amounts of time, and that had only gotten worse since Mariah died. I was all she had left with her parents across the country.

I narrowed my eyes at her, waving my fingers sadly. "We'll be fine, I promise. I'll be back before you know it."

"Can't wait," she whispered, trying to smile despite the undeniable sadness in her expression. I couldn't look at her any longer, or I may have changed my mind, may have said we should cancel the trip and stay home to binge Netflix with her instead. I turned away abruptly and grabbed at the door handle. I was buckling in as Ryan finally sank into his seat and started the car.

"You ready?" he asked, smiling at me with a boyish grin. I picked at the skin around my thumb.

"Mhm."

Noticing my nervous habit, he put his hand over mine, stopping me at once. "Everything's going to be fine. Trust me. You're going to love this place. It's so perfect—all the privacy we could ever want, gorgeous views, a hot tub, a fully stocked kitchen. It's pure paradise in the Smokies, at least according to the ad."

"I can't wait," I said, though it was a laughable lie. I hated going to new places. Hated doing anything new. Ryan blamed it on my anxiety, but the truth was that I just liked my space. I liked the comfort that came with familiarity.

He ran a thumb across my knuckles before pulling his hand away and tossing me his phone. "Want to choose the music?"

With that, we pulled slowly down the drive, and I scrolled through the music downloaded on his phone, searching for a song to put me at ease. It calmed me to have something I could control, and though I wasn't sure if that was why Ryan had done it, it was a sweet gesture.

I settled on an Ashley McBryde song and slid his phone into the cup holder, scooting down into the seat until I was more comfortable. I twisted the edge of my cardigan in my hands, staring out the window and resisting the urge to put my feet on the dash. Ryan would remind me that in a car crash, it would send my knees through my chest, so it was best not to even try it.

"Did you put the snacks where you can reach them?" he asked, glancing behind him.

I guess I could've told him that taking his eyes off the road was as dangerous as putting my feet on the dashboard, but instead I reached behind me and produced the bag of travel snacks we'd prepared. He stuck his hand inside, pulling out a handful of M&M's and popping them in his mouth.

We turned out of the subdivision and onto the highway out of town, and Ryan took my hand again. He lifted it to his lips and kissed my thumb. "Love you."

"I love you, too," I whispered.

"He's going to be fine. You know Everleigh will spoil him more than we do."

I nodded. I did know. Truth was, that wasn't the only reason I was nervous, but I hadn't worked up the nerve to tell him the rest yet. When we'd agreed to hold off on a honeymoon in order to save money—I refused to let his parents pay for the wedding *and* the honeymoon—it was also because of Stanley's ailing condition and my anxiety over traveling. It was why I was so grateful when Ryan told me where we'd be going this week.

A cabin in the woods, not far from home yet away from the hustle and bustle, was exactly the type of place I should've loved. Somewhere peaceful where I could relax. He knew me so well it was almost scary. He'd learned about me in an almost obsessive way, sometimes asking questions to the point that it felt somewhat like a pop quiz. He wanted to know me, wanted to know how I felt about things, what I thought, what I believed. It should've been flattering, but for an introvert who had trouble expressing herself, even to those closest to her, it was still a bit of a challenge.

Still, Ryan knew more about me than most people. But what he didn't know was that when we got to the cabin, the conversation waiting for us wasn't going to go well. I wasn't sure how he'd take my news—he'd be upset for sure, but just how upset? In the six months since we'd been married, I'd seen Ryan at his best. Patient. Kind. Loving.

But would that change?

If I told him I knew his darkest secret?

If I told him mine?

I didn't know, but I couldn't put either conversation off any longer. I had to be honest with him about everything, and this was the perfect time to do it. It was time for us both to face the truth.

CHAPTER THREE

Ryan

When we arrived at the cabin, Grace had calmed down a bit. She'd stopped wringing her fingers in her hands, stopped picking at the excess skin around her nails. That was progress. Slowly, and with time, I was learning the ways to calm her. Music, for one thing. Silence, for another. It might seem like the two are counterintuitive, but that wasn't the case for Grace. She listened to music the way some meditated. Quietly. She never sang along. She didn't dance. It was purely a reflective experience, and she soaked up every moment.

Guided by our GPS, I pulled down a long, gravel drive. I could see the cabin as we rounded the corner, and I breathed a sigh of relief. It was every bit as beautiful as in the pictures. The small, two-story cabin set back from the circular drive was surrounded on every side by thick woods with less than ten feet of cleared yard total. There was a small, covered porch that led to the front door, two solid wood posts running from floor to ceiling.

The cabin was built into the earth of the mountain, most of the bottom floor underground. From where we were, we could see a glimpse of the backside of the cabin, decks on each floor, with both running the entire width of the structure. The wood looked hand cut, with unique knots, patterns, and bumps in each piece. I pulled the car to a stop in front of the house, lowering the music from a volume too loud for me, and put the car in park. I waited, knowing it would take Grace a moment to pull from her trance, and when she did, she met my eyes.

There she was. My peaceful, stoic wife. The woman I'd fallen hard and fast for. The mysterious woman I couldn't seem to get enough of.

"We're here," I told her, nodding toward the cabin as if she hadn't noticed. She pulled out her phone, taking a quick picture of it.

"What are you doing?" I chuckled.

"Sending a picture to Everleigh to let her know we made it okay."

I frowned, pulling my phone off its dash mount and staring at the screen. "You'll have a hard time getting it to go through. There's terrible signal out here in the mountains."

She frowned, looking at her screen. "Ew, you're right. This really is out in the middle of nowhere." She let her phone drop to her lap and sat still, staring up at the house in awe. "It's beautiful, though." She should've been proud. It was a lot. Finding the perfect place at the perfect price point wasn't easy, but somehow I'd managed. I climbed from the car, my shoes crunching on the leaves and gravel beneath my feet.

"You haven't seen anything yet. And don't worry. It'll be fine," I told her. "I'm sure she knows we're okay."

"You're right. I was selfishly hoping to check in on Stanley."

"Yeah, I assumed that was the real reason. You aren't going to know what to do without Stanley snuggles for a week."

She giggled. "I guess I'll just have to settle for Ryan snuggles instead."

"I fart less often, if that makes you feel any better," I told her, making her laugh even harder.

"And give better kisses," she agreed. "Just don't tell him that."

My brows raised. "Happy to prove your point later."

"I'll take you up on it." She grinned at me warmly, inhaling as she pushed open her door and spun around. "Oh, Ryan, you weren't kidding. This place is incredible. It even smells like fall out here."

I had started to open the door to begin unloading our luggage, but I stopped, walking across the driveway toward her. She looked at me with a hesitant expression, a small smile playing on her lips, and I put my arms around her, pulling her in for a kiss. "*You're* what's incredible, you know that?"

She gave her head a half-shake, ready to deny it, but she didn't. That was progress, at least. It had taken me so long to get her comfortable with accepting how amazing she was—how beautiful, how smart, how thoughtful. I showered her with compliments, not because I had to, but because she deserved them. She deserved to feel loved every single day, and that was what I was going to do for her. She deserved everything. "I love you for doing this," she chose to say, instead of arguing that she wasn't incredible. *Progress.*

"But you're right. It's amazing here. Two stories, a hot tub, fully stocked kitchen and *bar.*" I wiggled my brows at her. "Plus, wait 'til you see the view from the second floor."

I handed her two of our lighter bags and lifted the largest suitcase, setting it down and pulling out the handle before grabbing the grocery bags we'd loaded with a myriad of snacks.

"I can carry something else," she protested.

"I've got these. Besides, I need you to open the door." We walked toward the house, past a small, black grill that had been built into the ground, and neared the two wooden steps that led to the porch. There was a cherry-stained wooden rocking chair to the right, just under a small, green mailbox that had been affixed to the siding and had the painted house numbers, 231. I moved slowly, trying to hide how much I was struggling under the weight of the bags as she stared around. Tennessee in the fall really was something to behold, and I was feeling the magic of experiencing it with her then.

"I've never been to the mountains," she said thoughtfully. "The air really is different up here."

"Yeah, it is," I agreed. "Fresher somehow. Crisp. Especially this time of year, and you can't beat the way the mountains look with the fog coming off them."

When we reached the door, I recited the code I'd memorized from the welcome email and waited for her to unlock it. She typed in the numbers on the small, gray keypad, and we heard a sharp click.

When she pushed the door open, we stepped inside the kitchen, and I placed the groceries on the small table. Because the house was built into the mountain, upon entering, we were already on the second floor. There was a flight of stairs to our right that led downstairs to the first floor. Nothing had changed from the pictures I'd seen online, and as someone who had once traveled often, that was refreshing to see. The kitchen was plain, nothing extravagant, but it would do. We made our way through the open-concept living room and turned to our left, into the bedroom, complete with a Jacuzzi tub next to the bed.

"Oh, babe!" she squealed. "This is *nice*."

It wasn't nice, not really. But it was what we could afford, and it would do just fine. I was dying to spoil her with extravagant trips of luxury, but without my parents' help, my small salary and commissions weren't going to allow for that anytime soon. It was one of Grace's conditions when we'd gotten married. That I had to stop taking the monthly allowance from my parents—the guilt money they showered me with in order to convince me my childhood hadn't been so bad after all. Giving up the money wasn't a hard decision. I'd choose Grace over anything, any person, any amount of money, every single day. And it was because of my problematic childhood that I'd been so determined to do better by her. Unlike my dad, I'd never cheat on her. Never choose work or women over my family. Grace was my entire world, and I was unapologetic over that.

I set our bags down and put a hand on her back, leading her into the living room once again and then out onto the deck. The second story of the cabin overlooked a section of sloping woods, a story below, nothing but changing leaves—all green, brown, and yellow—as far as the eye could see. In the distance, the Smoky Mountains were living up to their name, an ominous fog rising from in between the trees.

She sucked in a breath, not speaking for a while, enough to make me worry. "Do you like it?"

She looked at me, and I saw the hint of tears in her eyes then. "This is the nicest thing anyone's ever done for me."

Her words were a sucker punch to the gut, and I had to look away to process them. How was this cheap honeymoon in a rundown cabin as our six-months-late honeymoon the nicest thing anyone had ever done for her?

She deserved so much more. "Sweetheart, I've got to step up my game." I pulled her in for a hug then, still unable to meet her eye. Her expectations were depressing, honestly. She was simple and, while I wouldn't have changed a thing about her, I wanted her to expect more from me. She was so easy to please, but I didn't want to get complacent. I wanted to do better, impress her more.

"You do so much for me," she said simply, reading my mind.

"Not enough. It could never be enough."

She lowered her brow, running a finger across my chest. "You're intense sometimes, Ryan. You know that?"

"I know," I admitted. "I'm a lot." I always had been. It had been an issue with girls that I'd dated in the past, the real reason I hadn't married until I was thirty-seven. Not that I didn't want commitment, like Grace suspected, but that I wanted to commit too quickly. I was too much, too involved, too intense, too in love. But how could anyone be too obsessed with their wife? It wasn't possible. I only wanted to do the best I could by her. "Does it bother you?"

She shook her head, wrinkling her nose, her eyes full of warmth and love. "I knew who you were when I married you. I'm with you because of who you are. I wouldn't want you any other way. I can't imagine loving anyone else like I love you." She pressed up onto her toes and kissed me briefly. When she pulled away, I tugged her back to me, shaking my head as I lowered my mouth to hers again. I could've kissed her all day for the rest of my life and never gotten tired of it.

"I'm glad to hear you say that, because I'd never want you to love anyone else," I whispered when the kiss finally ended. I kept my face close to her, our skin practically touching. "Now, what do you say we grab some wine and relax in the hot tub?"

"You read my mind," she said, resting her head on my shoulder as if it carried the weight of the world. I kissed her temple, feeling like the luckiest guy in the world to get to shoulder that burden.

Twenty minutes later, we had settled into the hot tub, a small cooler with three bottles of wine—merlot for me, moscato for her, and a bottle of rosé that we'd both enjoy—resting on its side. I poured us each a glass and handed hers off.

Her face was stoic as she watched me take a drink. "Don't worry. I won't drink too much," I promised.

"I didn't say anything," she said, taking a sip of her own drink.

"I know what you're thinking," I said, winking at her.

"That my husband is so incredibly handsome?"

Warmth fluttered throughout my chest. "That your husband is so incredibly lucky to be here with his gorgeous wife is more like it."

Her cheeks pinkened as she glanced down humbly, hiding those emerald eyes behind thick lashes. When she looked back up, she played with a strand of her hair. "I love you, Ryan. I just want you to take care of yourself."

"I am," I promised. "I'm pacing myself. I just want to enjoy our honeymoon and, once we're back home, it's half a glass once or twice a week, and that's my limit." I put two fingers up. "Scout's honor."

She took another sip of her wine. "I know. I trust you."

"I love you for looking out for me, honey."

"I always will." The sun was setting into the horizon, casting a warm glow across her skin, and I couldn't help staring. "Are you missing work yet?" she asked, smirking playfully as she sipped her wine.

"Never when I'm with you," I promised. It was true, but uncomfortable. She looked away. There was that intensity again. I couldn't help myself. She'd always hated it when I was, in her words, 'sappy' because she wasn't. It wasn't that she was cold, but she felt things differently than I did. Our levels of comfort with our feelings differed greatly. While Grace had always been more reserved, I openly laid out the way I felt about everything. While I was affectionate all the time, there were days where she said she just didn't want to cuddle. Days when she'd rather not be touched. We were different. I was still learning her boundaries and how to break through them, and when to back off.

Before Grace, there were others. Other women I loved, other women who'd broken my heart. But I was determined not to let that happen with Grace. I'd forced myself to move as slowly as I could, to respect her space and the walls she had up. It pained me to do so, but she was worth it. I didn't have a choice when it came to her. She was special. She was different. She was my wife.

I'd tried to figure out what exactly it was that made her so different for quite a long time, but there was no solid, concrete answer. There rarely was with matters of the heart, or so I was learning. Grace was different from the others in that she depended on me more than they had. She needed someone to protect her, to care for her. To make her believe she was worthy of the bond we shared, of the love I had for her. Sticking around meant more to her because she'd never had anyone to do that.

In foster care most of her life after her parents, both addicts, died when she was young, Grace had never had a stable childhood. She'd never had anything stable, as a matter of fact. Not until she met me. She'd told me so often she'd never had anyone aside from Everleigh who had stayed a constant in her life, which was why she sometimes struggled with the intensity of our relationship. Her longest-standing relationship was with Everleigh, her best friend, then Stanley, her overweight Labrador, and then me. It was sad, and it was why I was determined to show her how love was supposed to be. How people were supposed to act when they were in love.

After we met, it had taken me six months to convince her to go out with me, then another six months to convince her to marry me, and up until I saw her walking down the aisle, I was sure she was going to leave me hanging. She had said things were moving too fast, but I didn't believe it. I wouldn't allow her to believe it. It felt like a snail's speed to me. I would've married her after our first date if it hadn't been crazy.

Like I said, I'm 'intense.' But that was our love. It was intense and passionate and life-altering. We were perfect, meant to be together. Eventually, she saw it, also. It was a good thing, too, because I'd damn near given up. But I couldn't give up. She needed me. She was counting on me. I was going to show her that love was supposed to feel this way. That she was safe with me. Loved. Taken care of. I could love her forever, and I planned to do exactly that.

"What are you thinking about?" she asked, and I shook my head, pushing the thoughts away. She thought of herself as so brave and independent, I could never let her know I thought any different. I couldn't let her know that I was sure her life would implode without me—and I knew mine would without her.

"What do you mean?"

"You seem… deep in thought. Anything in particular?" If she only knew.

"I was just thinking of all the fun we're going to have while we're here."

She seemed to like that answer. "Oh, yeah?"

"Yeah. I have some exciting things planned."

"Like what?" She inched forward in the tub, and I felt her hand brush my thigh. She placed herself in between my legs, stopping only when her face was mere inches from mine.

"Well,"—I wrapped my free hand around her waist, teasing her as I rambled on about normal things when all I really wanted to do was tear her bathing suit off right then and there—"we can go for a hike. There's a stream down in the woods from what the listing said, so maybe we can find it. And there's a little ice cream shop that we passed on the way in. That would be nice to try out."

"I wonder if they have salted caramel…" She touched her tongue to her upper lip.

"I'll bet they do." I licked my own, mirroring her without meaning to.

She laughed, flicking my nose and taking me out of the moment. At least she finally seemed at ease. "You're the best. Have I told you that lately?"

"I never mind hearing it," I said honestly, kissing her lips without warning. When we broke apart, I took another sip of my wine. "Happy honeymoon, babe."

"Happy honeymoon," she whispered, lowering her mouth to mine. I heard the clink of her glass as she set it on the edge of the hot tub, sliding further onto my lap. I put mine down, too, wrapping both arms around her. She pulled away, breathless, and rested her head on my shoulder.

"I'm never going to want to leave," she said thoughtfully.

"Who says we have to?" The thought of locking ourselves away from the rest of the world for a while was immensely tempting.

She shook her head, not responding. "Stanley will miss us too much."

I knew it was the opposite way around—that *she* would miss *him* too much instead—but I didn't argue. "Yeah, I guess you're right. We'll have to go home eventually." I paused, tucking a piece of hair behind her ears. "That doesn't mean we can't enjoy ourselves while we're here."

"Oh, I plan to..." She lifted her head and her glass, draining the remaining wine from it. I watched her throat bounce as she swallowed.

"Someone's thirsty," I joked, reaching for my own glass.

She ran her finger across her perfect lips. "Just trying to calm the last of my nerves from the drive, I think."

I lifted the drink to my own lips, but paused, lowering it. "Are you still feeling anxious? You seem okay."

"I am," she said quickly. "Mostly. You know how I get about new places."

"So, you don't like the cabin?"

Her eyes widened. "No, no. It's not that." She rested a hand on my chest, sending fire across my skin. "I love it here. Honestly, Ryan. It's—all I could've hoped for. You make it obvious how well you know me because I literally couldn't have picked anything better. I'm just weird about anything unfamiliar. You remember the first time I stayed over at your place, don't you?"

Of course, I did. She was up all night, pacing my living room, too nervous to sleep. Also, though I wouldn't point it out, it was *our* place now. "I'm sorry, sweetheart. I thought this was something nice for you. I don't want you to spend the whole time upset."

"It *is*. And I'm not. This place is so nice. I meant what I said: it's the nicest thing anyone's ever done for me, and I'm so grateful that you cared enough to do it. Honestly. This is my problem, not yours. I just need to settle in. By tomorrow, I'll be fine." She refilled her glass and knocked back most of it immediately. "Unless you could think of some way to"—a wrinkle formed on the bridge of her nose—"*de-stress* me."

I laughed under my breath, reaching for her. I cupped her arm, dragging her toward me as she feigned resistance. I wrapped my hand around the back of her head. "Now that you mention it, I think I've got a few ideas."

"You do, do you?" She gave in to my advances, leaning in as I reached for the tie of her bathing suit top. I gave it a tug, letting the top fall down and expose her breasts. Heat immediately spread through my body at the sight. She covered herself up instantly, her cheeks flaming red with embarrassment and too much wine.

"Ryan!" she cried. "You can't do that out here. What if someone saw?"

"What are you talking about? Who would see? There's no one out here!" I waved a hand toward the woods. She looked around, further proving my point as only the trees looked back. "Unless you count woodland creatures, we're all alone, babe." I slid further into the water, placing my hands over hers as I tried to pull them away. "Let me see you, please. I promise to make it worth your while."

To my relief, she frowned, but let her hands drop away, exposing herself wholly to me before she sank further into the water. "God, you're so beautiful." I never got tired of seeing her bare body, breasts and skin and places only I was allowed to see. I lifted my hand, rubbing it across her nipple gently. She looked out across the deck again.

"You're sure this is okay?"

"Trust me, babe," I whispered heatedly as I lowered myself further, preparing to submerge my head in the water. "No one can see us out here."

I went under the water then, blissfully unaware of how wrong I was.

CHAPTER FOUR

Grace

As darkness fell, we had only the glowing blue lights from underneath the water's surface in the hot tub and the dim porch light to keep us from fading into total oblivion—both from the wine and the pure black sky. People said you could see hundreds more stars in the sky once you left the city, but that didn't seem to be the case that night. It was like nothing existed but us and the moon.

And the wine.

My fingers were practically prunes, wrinkled and gross from being in the water too long. I hadn't bothered to put my top back on, much to Ryan's enjoyment. It lay next to his swimming trunks, dripping dry beside the three empty bottles of wine on the edge of the tub.

I sighed loudly, exhaustion beginning to set in. "I guess we should go in. It's getting late."

It took him a moment to respond; I watched his face change in the shadows. "I don't really want to move…"

"Me either, lazy bones. But I'm exhausted. It's been a long day."

"Okay," he said with a loud yawn.

"Besides that, I need my rest if you're planning to take me on a hike tomorrow." I stood, not sure why I was still talking when he'd already agreed, and grabbed my top, sliding it around my chest and tying it behind my neck.

He leaned forward sloppily, kissing the space between my breasts, then my collar bone and jawline. He stopped at my lips. "Let's get you to bed, then."

I grinned, stepping out of the hot tub and wrapping a towel around my waist. I hated the way my wrinkled fingers felt against the cotton of the towel, so I balled my fists up, trying to prevent touching them against anything until they dried. It was like nails on a chalkboard to me.

Ryan climbed out behind me, grabbing his wet trunks but not bothering to put them on as he wrapped his towel around his waist and put a hand on my back, leading me toward the door.

We trailed wet footprints across the wooden deck, stopping when we reached the glass door. I put a hand on the cool metal of the handle and turned.

Click.

I turned it again.

Click.

Then I dried my hands and turned it again.

Click.

When I looked over my shoulder at Ryan, he was staring at me in confusion. "Can you not get it?"

"It won't open. It's…" My words and thoughts came out slowly, almost somberly, thanks to the wine. "It's locked."

He nudged me out of the way, reaching for the handle. "It's not locked… It may just be tricky." I watched him turn the handle, but when he looked back at me, I knew he realized he had been wrong. It *was* locked. More importantly, we were locked out. "How did it get locked?" he demanded.

"I don't know, don't ask me. You were the last one out." I was suddenly feeling very sober indeed.

"No, I wasn't! You were!"

"No, Ryan, you left your towel on the couch and had to go back for it."

"No—" He paused, thinking. "I thought you… I don't remember, and it doesn't really matter. What matters is figuring out how to get back in. Do you have a hair pin or something?"

"What? You're going to pick the lock? How would you even know how to do that?"

"My cousins used to lock me out of the bedroom at my grandma's all the time. You learn things." He shrugged. "Do you have one?"

I put my hand to my hair, though the question was ridiculous. I hadn't had a bobby pin in my hair in years, and I certainly didn't have one at the moment. "No, of course I don't. How would it have even gotten locked? It doesn't make any sense."

"Maybe we accidentally turned the lock when we shut it. I don't know!" He growled, hitting his hand on the wood of the door in panic. He glanced around, our good mood vanishing.

"What do we do?" I asked, watching as reality set in on his face. "Can we call someone? The property management company? A locksmith?"

"I don't have my phone out here. We left them inside." He put a hand to his forehead, staring off into the darkness. "I'm going to have to climb down and go around and open the door with the keypad." He walked toward the edge, looking over the railing.

"Do *what*? You can't be serious." I made my way to him, touching his back as I followed his line of vision. In the daytime, we could see down. I knew the ground was there, the forest below, but at that point, there was nothing but darkness as far as the eye could see. A lump formed in my throat. "Ryan, you can't. You've been drinking, and it's pitch black out here. What if you get hurt? I'd be up here all alone without a way to help you. There could be wolves or… God, bears in the woods. We have to be smart about this, and climbing down from the second story into a forest we can't see isn't smart."

"What do you suggest, then?" he asked dryly. "We can't just stay out here all night."

I sighed. "That's exactly what we have to do." There was no other way.

"What? Just stay out here forever? We have no food. No way to go to the bathroom. We're going to get eaten alive by mosquitoes."

"Not forever. Just for the night. I think we can survive without food for a few hours. We have to. We can ride out the night out here, and then, in the morning when we can see better, you can climb down. At least that way you can see what you're doing."

He shook his head. "It's going to get cold tonight." As if to prove his point, the wind howled, and I wrapped my towel around me to hide my shiver.

"Not freezing, just cool. We'll cuddle up in our towels, and if we get too cold, we can get back in the hot tub." I patted his shoulder. "Come on, it's not ideal, but it's our only option right now."

After a moment of contemplation, he nodded begrudgingly. "Fine. You're probably right."

"I *am*."

He pulled me in for a hug, and I wrapped my towel partially around us both. "I'm sorry I blamed you. I was just stressed."

"It's okay, babe. You don't need to apologize to me. I know you didn't mean it. It's all going to be okay. We've had too much to drink, we're tired, and this is more than a little stressful. We'll figure it out tomorrow."

"You're the perfect amount of calm when I need it most," he whispered, kissing the top of my head. "I don't know what I'd do without you."

"Apparently fall from second-story balconies and break your arm," I said playfully. "Now, come on, we can curl up in the rocking chairs and try to get some sleep. At this point, I'm pretty sure I could sleep anywhere."

We made our way to the chairs, scooting them forward across the deck until they were close to the wooden railing so we could rest our feet on the top. It wasn't the most comfortable thing, but it was better than sitting up straight. Ryan put his trunks on before he sat down, and we situated the towels over as much of our bare skin as possible, trying to keep warm in the crisp, fall breeze.

It was peaceful out there, despite our predicament. An owl hooted overhead as I began to doze off, ignoring the painful way the wood of the chair dug into my skin. I'd slept in less comfortable places and positions, so I wasn't worried. I'd been made of stone, able to withstand just about anything. Ryan, on the other hand, had lived a cushy life of privilege and wealth. I was sure he'd never slept anywhere but his memory foam mattresses, underneath Egyptian cotton. Be that as it may, he didn't complain.

My sweet husband had never been a moaner. He went with the flow in every situation, including this one. His only complaints were generally on my behalf. I heard him shift in the chair, wrapping the towel around him once again when it fell away, and as I was drifting off in an alcohol-fueled slumber, I heard his voice. "Grace?"

I couldn't be bothered to open my eyes. "Yeah?"

"Just so you know, I was going to rock your world tonight."

"Mhm."

"Raincheck?"

If I wasn't so tired, I would've laughed at his sleepy, drunk ramblings. "Raincheck."

I never had the chance to take him up on that.

CHAPTER FIVE

Ryan

When I woke up, my body was sore and uncomfortable. My hair had dried stiffly from the chlorine in the hot tub, and I had the painful imprints of the rocking chair on my skin. I stood and stretched, remembering our problem at once.

Grace was awake, staring at me thoughtfully from her chair. She seemed tired, and I wondered how well she'd slept. Despite the uncomfortable chair, I'd slept like a baby. The same couldn't be said for her, it appeared. I took in her soft skin, her deep, ocean-like green eyes.

"Mornin' beautiful."

Her cheeks pinkened, bringing life to her face. "Morning."

"How did you sleep?"

"Not well," she admitted, confirming my suspicions. "I kept worrying that you'd try to climb down the side of the house once I fell asleep."

I furrowed my brow. "I promised you I'd wait until this morning."

"I know," she said, "and that doesn't make me feel any better. It's so dangerous, Ryan."

I scoffed, trying to seem braver than I felt at the thought. "I'll be fine, honestly. I used to do rock climbing in college; this can't be much different." I'd never admit it, but I'd dropped rock climbing after four classes because I was so terrified of heights.

She nodded; no fight left in her. "I just don't want you to get hurt."

The morning was muggy, the sun beginning to appear over the horizon and bringing with it humidity that had my skin slick with sweat. I smelled terrible, my mouth was dry from drinking too much, my jaw was sore from sleeping without my nightguard, and my contacts had dried to my eyeballs. Truth be told, there was very little I'd wanted more in my life than to get inside the house. No matter the cost.

I stood up, laying my towel back in the chair and walking toward the railing. As I looked down the one-story drop below into a steep slope of ground that led to a dense forest, I felt my heart accelerate. If I swung over the top of the railing, I could maneuver my way down the railing, but then it was a several-foot drop to the ground-floor patio and then I could walk straight around the house. No problem.

Although, the house *was* on a steep slope. If I wasn't careful about my landing, I'd end up rolling down the hill and into the forest without the ability to stop. And that was only the worst case if I didn't manage to break something—or several somethings—on the way down.

I looked around. We had two towels, but nothing else to make a makeshift rope for me to slide down on. It would never reach the patio below. We could try to throw the hot tub cover down to cushion my fall, but the chances I'd hit the small square of padding were slim. There were no houses for miles, no one to hear our cries for help. There was no other choice—I had to accept it. I had to convince her this was it.

When I looked back to where she'd been standing, she was gone. I spun completely around, noticing she'd gone back toward the door. "What are you doing?" I asked.

She had the end of my sunglasses, trying to stick the end of the temple into the lock. "There has to be a way to get back inside without doing this."

I hurried toward her, reaching for the glasses. "*Don't.* There isn't. We aren't going to be able to pick the lock with those. You'll just end up bending or breaking them." She stopped, looking at me like she was going to argue, but handed them to me instead.

"I just don't want you to fall, and Ryan, you're *going* to fall. You aren't Spiderman."

"I'd look good in his suit though, right?" I joked, brushing fake dust from my shoulders in an attempt to get her to smile.

"I'm worried less about his suit than a full-body cast," she said. I had let her down. I knew it. She was disappointed that I couldn't figure a way out of this. I was disappointed in myself. Our first night and, already, I'd managed to get us into the most ridiculous situation. Even if I did manage to get down without breaking a bone, this was sure to put a damper on the trip.

I put my hand on the knob, ready to rattle it open in frustration, and to my surprise—

Click.

The knob twisted.

The door opened.

The cool air from inside the cabin hit us.

"What the—" Grace looked at me, her jaw slack. "How did you—did you break it?"

"No," I said, then looked at the knob to be sure. "I don't think so. It just opened."

"How is that possible? Did I actually unlock it somehow?" She glanced at the sunglasses in my hand.

"No way…" I trailed off, because there was no logical explanation. Unless… "Maybe the handle just sticks, and we were too drunk last night to realize it." I scratched the back of my neck.

"We hadn't been drinking *that* much," she argued, looking around the empty living room and then back at the deck.

"Well, maybe you did pick it, then. Somehow." I ran a thumb across the metal edge of my sunglasses. It just didn't make sense.

I stepped over the threshold, and she followed suit, both of us confused as ever. "I guess it doesn't matter. We're inside now, and I need a shower. Wanna join me?"

She nodded, closing the door and turning the lock. She unlocked it, then relocked it, testing the doorknob. It was locked this time for sure. "Desperately."

CHAPTER SIX

Grace

The woods were treacherous that afternoon as a heatwave made its way through the area. Our hike was stiflingly hot and humid, and filled with overgrown weeds, buzzing insects, and obscure tree roots that seemed to jump out of nowhere and trip my step. We lumbered through, quickly downing the water we'd packed, despite our best intentions to make it last.

Though I had many complaints, it was undeniably beautiful. The rapidly changing leaves were further proof that my favorite season was coming, as much as the day's temperatures tried to convince me I was wrong. The tranquility of the woods provided us much-needed solace, space to clear our heads and let go of our worries.

"There's a stream up here," Ryan said, panting up ahead of me. I wasn't sure if he was planning to get a drink or go for a swim, but I nodded either way, my parched throat preventing me from talking more than necessary.

He slowed his step, holding out his hand, when I heard the sound of the rushing water. "Can you grab the straws from the side of my backpack? If I don't get something to drink soon, I feel like I'm going to pass out."

"Yep, hold still." I unzipped the side pocket of his dark gray bag, reaching for the LifeStraws near the bottom. I'd thought they were a silly purchase when he'd ordered them. We weren't planning to hike intensely, and I thought we'd have plenty of water. Now, as our supply of water had dwindled just an hour into our hike, I was glad I hadn't voiced those opinions. I held the blue tube in my hand, incredibly thankful to have it. When we grew nearer to the stream, he stopped abruptly, his hand out in front of me to force me to stop, too.

"H-hello," he said. I looked up, my eyes almost permanently locked on the forest floor to keep from stumbling over stray rocks and tree roots—my knees couldn't bear to take much more of a beating than they already had—and tried to conceal my gasp.

There was a ragged, orange tent up ahead of us, several holes torn in the top of it, just steps away from the stream. In front of it, a shirtless man sat just beyond the remnants of a fire in the dirt, a black circle with small, charred twigs that had long since burned out. He had wild, dirty gray hair and a beard that stuck out in every direction. His face was tanned dark, with deep wrinkles around his eyes and mouth. He appeared filthy, his bare feet were covered in bleeding sores, and his jeans were stained with dirt and terribly frayed at his ankles. Near the fire's remains lay an empty can of tuna, and to the right of that he had a small supermarket basket of used cans. There was a line of some sort hanging between two trees, where a sweat-stained T-shirt and a towel, that was more hole than cloth, hung.

His eyes were beady but tired, hidden beneath unkempt brows. He narrowed them at Ryan, completely disregarding me, and I felt a chill run down my spine. My breathing caught, and I felt my vision begin to tunnel, frozen in place. He hardly moved when Ryan spoke, instead looking back down at the ground.

"Sorry to bother you. Are you okay?" Ryan asked, and I found myself able to move again, fear coursing through me. I tugged at his arm. "Are you hurt?"

"Ryan, come on," I whispered, my heart rate accelerating. I felt as though I might pass out, though my husband clearly hadn't noticed my fear. We needed to leave. Right then.

The man looked up at us again. His gaze fell to me finally. Then Ryan. He stood abruptly, and I winced, unable to slow my heart. Panic gripped at my organs, raging through my body as I tried to decide how we would escape. We were completely alone with this man.

We should leave. We should leave right now. No one knows where we are. No one knows where to find us. If I don't come home, what will happen to Stanley?

"Sorry to disturb you," Ryan said again. "I thought you might need some assistance. Are you camping or…?" He trailed off, the answer, that he was homeless, was obvious. Still, the man didn't speak. His shoulders rose and fell with heavy breaths as he darted his gaze between us, his face expressionless. "Do you live out here? Are you hungry? We have food—snacks. We don't have anything to drink, but—" He slung his backpack around his side and unzipped the top, producing packs of trail mix, crackers, and beef jerky. "Do you like any of this stuff?" He looked up as a lump formed in my throat. I squeezed my hands into fists, feeling my throat grow tight as I watched the man carefully. *Why can't he sense how wrong this all feels?*

"Here," Ryan offered, despite the man's silence. He held out the food, but the man didn't move. Didn't speak. Finally, Ryan placed the food on the ground, directly in between us and the man. His gaze fell to the ground, taking in the sight of the food, but he didn't budge. Ryan took a step back, giving him more space and forcing me back with him.

"You can have it," Ryan said. "We won't hurt you. I have sunscreen, too… Do you have any? The sun can get pretty bad out here." Again, he reached in his bag and produced the bottle of sunscreen. He tossed it next to the food, clouds of dust billowing out around it as it landed. "I'm sorry I don't have anything to drink." He looked at the two straws in our hands, turning his over in his palm before nodding, as if he was convincing himself.

I was frozen in place, unable to move, unable to think, unable to catch my breath. Why couldn't he see we were in danger? *Why can't he see we need to run?*

Upon seeing the man, the first thought I'd been able to form was that we should search for a path home that was quick, but not direct. We didn't want him to know where we were staying. Ryan's first thought was to empty our bags voluntarily.

Ryan held the straw near his lips as if he were demonstrating how it worked before talking to the man again. "You know what? Here you go. You probably need this more than we do." He held it out. When the man still didn't reach for it, he said, "It's called a LifeStraw. I'm not sure if you've heard of them, but they're really handy. You can drink water from the stream, and it purifies it for you. *Makes it safe to drink.* It's used, I tried it out when we got them, but we've washed it... Would you like it?"

The man's jaw tightened as he stared at the straw, still not speaking. His head jerked down, only slightly, and back up. A barely noticeable nod.

"All right, cool. Here you go. It's all yours." He held it out even further, but the man didn't budge, so he stepped forward and laid it with the pile he'd formed. "I have a little bit of cash, too. Not much, but..." He reached into his pocket, pulling out two twenty-dollar bills and a handful of ones—most of the cash he had on him. He dropped them into the pile. "Hopefully it will help you."

The man blinked, staring down at the pile, then back up. Ryan laughed awkwardly. "You're probably ready for us to get out of your hair, huh? Do you mind if we get a drink here, first? With her straw? We ran out of the water we packed." He gestured toward the stream.

"*No, Ryan,*" I whispered sharply. "We should go." My face burned hot with terror and adrenaline. No way in hell was I walking past the man toward the stream. We needed to leave. *Now.*

Ryan looked back at me, and he must've noticed the fear then, maybe for the first time, because he said, "O-okay. Well, never mind. We've got to go." He took a step back as I did, and to my relief, the man remained still. "Enjoy that, okay? And take care." He turned abruptly, but I didn't dare take my eyes off the man. Not until we were far enough gone that he was just a speck in between the trees, disappearing more with each step. Although he was soon swallowed by the woods surrounding him, I somehow couldn't shake the feeling that, wherever he was, he was still watching me.

Back at the cabin, my adrenaline had finally calmed down, though I still felt the nagging sensation of being on edge. We'd snuggled onto the couch, watching a silly romcom to relax. Ryan loved all things Ryan Reynolds, and his favorite way to spend an afternoon was watching one of his movies. Normally, I'd read a book or scroll aimlessly through my phone, but that afternoon, I desperately needed to laugh. So, I focused on the TV with all I had, unable to enjoy it because I was too busy trying to focus. I had my back against the arm of the couch, and his body was draped across mine, his head resting on my stomach.

"What's wrong?" he asked, looking up as I stopped running my fingers through his hair rhythmically.

I resumed. "Sorry, nothing."

"Are you falling asleep?"

"No, I was just thinking…" We hadn't talked about it much since we'd been home, too preoccupied with rehydrating and showering away the sweat in all our creases. "What do you think that man was doing out there?"

"The homeless guy?" he asked, a brow cocked, as if it hadn't been on his mind at all. How could it not have been? It was all I could think of. I nodded, and he said, "I guess that's where he lives. I mean, when you think about it, it's not the worst place, is it? He had the tent for shelter and the stream to drink from, wash his clothes in, and bathe in. Plus, way out here in the woods with no one to bother him, it's the perfect place. There's no one around for miles."

I swallowed at the thought, feeling uneasy. "But what do you think he does for food? I mean, I didn't see a fishing pole, and we're miles from the nearest town."

He ran a finger over my leg. "Yeah, you're right. I mean, he probably gets some food from the trash of the cabins in this area, but other than that, I'm not sure what he does. Maybe we should bring him more before we leave."

"No," I said, probably too quickly.

He stared at me. "Why not?"

I hesitated, unable to explain the way I felt to my blissfully oblivious husband. "I just don't like the way he was staring at us. It made me uncomfortable. He could be dangerous. And why wouldn't he talk? It just... freaked me out."

He scoffed, propping himself up on his elbows. "Why? I don't know why he didn't talk... Maybe he was shy. Maybe he was sick. Maybe he was just as worried about us as we were him."

"*Were* you actually worried?" I asked, furrowing my brow. "It didn't look like it. You seemed all too happy to give away all of our stuff to him."

"Are you mad about that?" He waited for my answer, but I couldn't give it. Though it was at the bottom of the list of reasons for my nervousness, the truth was, it did bother me that Ryan had no idea how it felt to be poor. To horde what little you had because you never knew when you'd need it. We weren't hurting financially now; we had much more than I'd ever had growing up, but we still didn't have much. I knew he felt safe, cushioned, because his parents could bail us out at any moment, but I didn't want to count on that.

I believed we should've held onto what we had. We could've offered a bag of trail mix, sure, but not *everything* we had. *What if we need it?* We'd have to go buy more now if we ever wanted to hike again. Not that I'd want to do that, not with that man out there. Maybe my experience should've made me kinder toward people in the same situation I'd once been in, but it hadn't. I wanted to make sure we were taken care of. If that made me heartless, so be it. I never wanted to struggle again. "We can just buy more. He needed it more than we do, Grace. I had to help him."

"You don't know that, though. For all you know, he could've just been camping, and you gave him *so* much stuff. He didn't even ask for it."

"Yeah, but you saw how he was living. And you're right, maybe he didn't need it. He could've been shy. Or camping. But, you know, it wasn't like… I mean, why does it matter? If he didn't need it, no harm done. If he did, great. What's your point? I guess I'm not understanding what you're so upset about. What did I do wrong? It wasn't like I gave him hundreds of dollars' worth of stuff. I can buy myself a new LifeStraw. My mother always said when you have a lot, you should give a lot, so that's what I try to do. You know that."

I did know that; he was right. I knew he donated to charities and dropped change into the Salvation Army buckets at Christmas time. What I didn't know was that he also made the habit of striking up conversations with dangerous strangers and then offering them all our food and money.

I put a finger to my temple, trying to articulate how I was feeling. Frustrated. Angry. Afraid. I felt like he'd put us in danger, and he didn't seem to realize it. "It's not about the straw, or anything you gave him. I just felt really unsafe, and I wanted to leave, but you weren't listening to me. We were out there all alone with a strange man. For all you knew, he could've been dangerous. He could've tried to hurt us."

"Oh, honey…" he said breathily. "I'm sorry for not realizing you were worried about that. You were safe with me. He didn't try to hurt us. He didn't do anything. I wasn't even thinking about you being worried or… afraid." He paused, glancing down. "But we made it back just fine, didn't we? We're safe. I'm still not really sure what you're upset with me about."

I took a breath, shoving my shaking hands under my thighs. "I'm not upset with you, Ryan. I just wish you were more aware of things sometimes."

He gave me a pitiful look. "Aware of things? You know I would've protected you. I wouldn't let anything happen to you. I was just trying to do a good thing."

"I know, sweetheart. I know you were, and God knows I love you for your kindness, but my point is, you could've put us in more danger. All I'm saying is, just because you're a big tough guy, doesn't make *me* any less in danger around men. I know guys don't have to worry so much about that kind of thing, but women do. *I do.* To a woman, coming across a strange man in the woods, or anywhere for that matter, is utterly terrifying. I was petrified that something awful would happen," I admitted.

His expression hardened. "Did you ever think that maybe I was doing what I did *because* I thought it might keep you safer? Because maybe if we'd seen him and walked away, he would've gotten angry and tried to take our stuff. But because I offered it to him, because I was kind to him, maybe that protected us."

I pressed my lips together. Maybe he was right. Maybe he and I had the same goal but had reacted in opposite manners. Perhaps I'd put us in more danger than he had, after all.

"I'm sorry. I don't know why I'm so shaken," I conceded, dropping my head onto the pillow behind it. He reached for my hand, pulling it out from under my thigh.

"It's okay. You don't have to explain yourself. You know that. I just don't want you to be mad at me or think I was trying to put you in any danger. I love you. I don't know what I'd ever do if something happened to you. I'd never forgive myself."

"I know. I know that. I'm sorry for being upset… I love you, too," I whispered as he pressed his lips to my knuckles.

"I'm going to take care of you forever, you know that?"

"I do," I said, my voice low as I felt the weight of the words I'd said to him at the altar not so long ago.

"I can't wait for us to have a little family." His gaze trailed from my eyes to my stomach and back. "Do you think it's too early for you to take the pregnancy test?" he asked, and the ever-present knot in my chest grew larger.

"Yeah, I do, Ryan. It takes at least two weeks before it would show positive even if we were…" I watched his hopeful expression fall, and I adjusted on the couch. "I actually wanted to talk to you about that." Two days before we'd left for vacation, he'd suggested we talk to a specialist if this month's attempt to conceive didn't succeed, obviously frustrated with how long it was taking us to get pregnant. I wasn't aware six months was considered *long*.

"Okay…" He reached for the remote and muted the TV, sitting up with concern on his expression.

I didn't want to do this right then. Not the first real day of the vacation. I'd intended to talk to him about it before our trip was over, but it had to be done right then. I had my window, and I had to take it. It was especially hard when he'd gone out of his way to do something nice for me, when we were supposed to be having a good time, but I had to tell him the truth. I couldn't put it off any longer. I had to admit to him that what he wanted and what I wanted were two very different things. I'd never tell him about the birth control pills I still took, but it was time for this dream to end. Besides, it was the easier of the two conversations I desperately needed to have with him on this vacation.

"It's about getting pregnant right now." My hands were in my lap then, and I looked down at them, trailing one hand's fingers over the other's palm. He waited. "I'm just not sure that… that we're ready."

Or that I'll ever be. I'd promised him I'd come off the pill in the weeks before our wedding, in time for my system to get regulated. He wanted to start trying for a child on our wedding night. I'd preferred to wait a few years. So why hadn't I just come out and said that? Truth was, I didn't know. What I did know was that I'd do just about anything to keep him thinking the sun rose and set with me, when, in reality, I was so incredibly flawed. No one had ever looked at me the way he did. I didn't want that to end.

So, I'd lied and said I'd stopped taking the pill. The doctor said it could take months for my cycle to return to normal after I stopped taking it, so Ryan was delighted when my next period came right on time. He thought it meant it would happen quickly.

But I still wasn't pregnant. I knew birth control wasn't fool-proof. I knew plenty of women who'd gotten pregnant on it, so each month I waited on pins and needles for my period to come, same as he did. Each month, without fail, it did. It wasn't fair to either of us for me to keep lying to him, I knew. He deserved to know the truth, no matter how afraid I was of his reaction. I couldn't put myself or my husband through the waiting and the wondering and the hoping anymore. I had to tell him, and I had to tell him now.

He was silent for a moment, as if waiting for me to go on, but finally, he cleared his throat. "I... sorry, I don't understand. What do you mean we aren't ready? You don't think I'd make a good dad?"

"*No*, it's not that at all. Honestly. You'll make an excellent dad someday, Ryan. I know that. It's just, well, I'm not positive when I want to have kids, and that seems like such a big decision to rush into. I'm sorry I didn't say anything sooner."

"We're married," he said, giving me a dry laugh. "How is it rushing? Having kids is the next logical step, right?"

"Says who? I know that's what society says, but honestly, is that what you want? Don't you want to have some time with each other before we bring a kid into the mix?"

"I mean, sure, but even once you get pregnant, we'd still have nine months with just us…"

I sighed heavily. "It's not the same."

"My parents had so much trouble getting pregnant with me, and they said I only made their relationship stronger. They couldn't have any more kids after me, no matter how hard they tried. I want a whole litter of kids. You know that." He smiled sadly. "The older they got, the less chance they had. We're already so much older than they were when they had me… The sooner we do this, the easier it'll be. Not just to conceive, but labor, too. And raising them. I don't want to be too old to play with our kids. My mom says having me was the best part of their marriage. I just want that. I want us to have what they had, the happiness of raising a family while we're young enough to enjoy it, without the struggle of fertility treatments and—"

"Yeah, I know, Ryan. I know the struggles your parents had made their marriage worse, and I know how much they wanted you… but not everyone has that. Not everyone has parents who love them or want them or know what to do with them… and just because they had trouble getting pregnant doesn't mean we will, and—" I was hyperventilating, my vision clouding with tears. He jumped into action, wrapping me in his arms as he rocked back and forth, and I closed my eyes, breathing in his heavy, woodsy cologne.

"Whoa, hey, slow down. Calm down. Easy… My parents were far from perfect. They wanted me, sure, but by the time I came along, things were already so bad between them… I'm not trying to compare us to them. That's not what I'm saying at all. I don't want what they had. I want what *we* have. We don't have to do anything you aren't ready for. You know that, don't you? I'm sorry you felt like you couldn't talk to me about this. I'm so sorry. Just… don't cry, okay? God, Grace. I feel like a jackass. I thought this was what you wanted."

I dabbed my eyes, though the tears continued to fall. "I thought it was, too. I don't know what I want—"

"Except me?"

I smiled, but it was small. "Except you."

"Then that's all that counts." He brushed a strand of hair from my face.

The sigh came, and I wondered why I'd let the conversation build up in my head so much. I knew my husband. I knew the man I'd married and how much he loved me. Did I really believe he loved the idea of a child more?

He patted my leg. "I want to have a baby with you, Grace. More than anything. I want our little family, the picket fence, the whole nine yards. But I only want that if it's something *you* want, too. I'm okay with keeping you to myself for a few more months... even, I mean, we could wait a whole year, if that's what it takes for you to be comfortable. I want our timing to be perfect." He ran his finger underneath my chin. "I got the girl of my dreams to marry me. That's all I care about. Let's give it a few months and come back to this. Maybe even a year, like I said. What do you say?"

A year sounded like the least amount of time it would take for me to be comfortable with the discussion, but I didn't want to push the argument any further. He was already giving me more than I'd expected. Perhaps an argument would've been easier—a screaming brawling match where I could've stood my ground and forced my point—but I'd never get that with Ryan. He'd proven time and time again that his calm was his entire personality. There was nothing else. I'd rarely seen him stressed and even less often seen him angry. It just wasn't in him.

"Thank you," I whispered, patting his cheek and then pressing my lips into the spot where my hand had been.

He nodded. "Always, sweetheart. I love you." His warm gaze met mine, and I felt the love in his eyes. "Now, not to ruin the mood, but I need to take a leak. Need anything while I'm up?"

I shook my head, snort-laughing as I watched him trot away from the couch and into the bedroom. I leaned my head back on the pillow, feeling overwhelmed with gratitude. Now, I could toss out the test that had been taunting me from its place in the suitcase. I could already feel the tension leaving my shoulders at the thought.

I pushed myself up, deciding on a glass of wine to celebrate. Who cared if it was not yet five in the evening? We were on vacation. We were celebrating, and I was allowed a drink.

I made my way into the kitchen, pulling open the cabinet to draw two glasses from its shelves. When I turned around, I jolted, dropping the glasses to the ground with a sharp shriek. The glass shattered at my feet, but I couldn't move. I stood frozen in place, staring out the large window that overlooked the sink toward the edge of the woods.

He was there.

The man from the woods.

Looking up at the house.

Watching us. Watching *me.*

I was frozen in place, my body trembling in fear. When I heard the toilet flush, the bathroom door open, and his footsteps heading my direction, I looked over to see him exiting the bedroom and rushing toward me.

"What is it? What's wrong? What happened?" He noticed the floor, now covered in shards of glass. "Are you hurt? Are you okay?"

"I—he is out there!" I pointed to the window with a trembling hand. "He followed us back! He's watching the house!"

"What are you talking about?" Ryan asked, reaching for my arm to pull me back away from the broken glass. "Watch your step."

"The man from the woods," I shrieked, looking back out the window. My heart sank. Ryan stepped up into the place where I'd been, grabbing the red broom out from between the refrigerator and the sink.

"Where is he? Are you sure?" He looked out the window, too, but it was no use. The man was gone. Startled, probably, by my shriek.

I looked out the window, shaking my head. "He was down there. Right down there. At the edge of the woods."

Ryan held his line of vision for a moment longer, then looked down at the floor where the glass remained. "Keep back. I don't want you to get cut." He began sweeping up the mess I'd made without complaint. "I don't see him out there. You probably just saw a deer or something. The woods are so thick, it's hard to tell, especially from this distance. It could have been your imagination playing tricks on you because you're worried about it."

"It wasn't a deer," I argued without power, my fingers to my lips, but he was no longer listening. He cleaned up the glass quickly, refusing to debate whether I'd been wrong, but I knew what I saw.

He was still out there. Just beyond the trees.

He'd followed us home.

He was watching.

CHAPTER SEVEN

Grace

That night after dinner, the world had gone dark, the cabin lit only by a lamp in the living room and a small light over the kitchen sink. I was standing in the kitchen, putting our salad into Tupperware when I heard the noise. A slow and steady scratch somewhere I couldn't pinpoint.

Scraaaatch.

Scraaaatch.

Scraaaatch.

Ryan headed my direction, the dish of lasagna in his hands.

"Do you want me to put this in—"

"Shhh! Shhh!" I cried, frozen in place. His eyes widened, his face growing pale.

"What's wro—"

"Shhh!" I told him, putting my finger to my lips. I waited, the sound of the clock on the wall louder than ever as we stood in nearly complete silence otherwise. He looked over his shoulder, a horror-stricken expression on his face. I didn't hear it anymore, but I hadn't imagined it. I knew that much. "You didn't hear that?"

He shook his head, his voice a low whisper. "Hear what?"

"That scratching noise…" I scratched the air with my hand. "It sounded like—"

Scraaaatch.

Scraaaatch.

Scraaaatch.

Scraaaatch.

"Like that!" I spun around, trying to decide where it was coming from.

Ryan cocked his head to the side, and for just a moment, I was sure he was going to tell me he hadn't heard a thing. Instead, he said, "What *is* that?"

I shook my head, making my way across the kitchen. "It sounds like an… an animal, maybe. Do you think this place has mice?"

Ryan set down the food and began opening up cabinets, moving things to and fro. "They'd better not."

I made my way toward the door, reaching to turn on the light above the table. As my hand touched the switch, I heard something different. Not scratching, but steady breathing. Deep, rhythmic, menacing breathing. *"What the—"* I flinched and flipped on the switch, immediately realizing it was the wrong one. Behind me, the glass of the door lit up as the porch light came on, and I screamed, shocked to see the dark outline of a figure standing just beyond the glass.

Ryan turned around, his eyes locked on me, then up at the door. "What was that?"

In a flash, the figure was gone, but I knew what I'd seen. "It was that man!" I cried, pointing toward the door as I backed away. "He was there. How long has he been here?"

"Now, calm down…" he said calmly. "We don't know that's what it was."

"You saw the shadow, didn't you? You saw him through the glass; you had to have!" I couldn't believe it. Was he really suggesting it could be anything else?

"I saw *something,* but it looked like a shadow more than anything. It could've been a tree—"

"There's no sun outside! How could a tree's shadow have looked like that?"

"Okay, well, maybe it was, like, a bear or something. We're in the mountains, right?"

"It wasn't a bear, Ryan!" I told him, shaking my head. "It was that man. He was out there. I told you I saw him out there in the woods earlier, and I just saw him again. I could hear him breathing through the door when I was standing next to it."

Ryan's jaw dropped. "I don't know… I hate to say it, but I think you're just maybe a little paranoid right now, sweetheart."

It felt like a slap in the face. I knew what I'd seen. Why was he so hell-bent on denying it? Why didn't he believe me? My expression must've shown my devastation, because without me saying a word, he smiled, reaching for my hand. I didn't give it to him.

"I'll tell you what." He grabbed a flashlight from the top of the refrigerator. "I'll go out there and check it out, okay? I'll show you it was nothing."

I frowned. "I don't want you to go out there. Even if it was a just bear, how would you defend yourself?"

He lifted the blind on the window over the sink, and I held my breath, waiting to see what he'd see out there. When he turned around, he was obviously feeling very pleased with himself. "See, nothing. No one's out there." He moved past me cautiously, nodding. "It's fine." He turned the lock, pulling the door open slowly, and I wondered if he could hear my heart pounding from there.

"Please don't go out there, Ryan," I whispered, my voice whiny and trembling. "Please."

It was too late. He opened the door wider, so I could get a good look at the porch. The *empty* porch. Moths buzzed around the porch light, which gave off a steady hum. "See, nothing here. No one. It could've been a bear. Maybe that's what the scratching noise was. Remember I showed you that video on Facebook of the bear who rang the doorbell?" He was moving to shut the door, but I was no longer listening. Instead, my gaze was locked on the doormat, my stomach churning. "It was probably just looking for food, and your scream scared it off."

I could hardly breathe.

"Do you think a bear left that?" I whispered, pointing my shaking finger toward the book lying on the welcome mat.

"What the... What the hell is that?" He leaned forward, picking up the hardback with two outstretched fingers.

"Leave it," I warned, though it was too late. He closed the door, latching the lock and tossing it on the counter as if it were contaminated. Whether it was or not, I felt it was. I clutched my stomach, trying to steady my breathing.

"Was this there before?"

I shook my head, my throat tight with words I couldn't bring myself to say.

"Maybe we just missed it. Whoever checked out last could've dropped it while they were leaving, and we didn't notice it until now."

I didn't argue, could barely breathe. Why was he so adamantly denying what was incredibly obvious? The man had been there. He'd left this for us. But why?

"Or maybe there was someone out there, and they found this and thought it was ours? Maybe the man thought it was ours, and that's why you saw him in the woods." He was rambling, but it made no sense. "Maybe he was bringing it back to you."

"That doesn't make sense. It took him hours to make it from the edge of the woods to the porch?" I refused to meet his eye as anger and panic swelled in my chest, competing for space. "Besides, if that were the case, why wouldn't he have knocked?"

"I told you, he could be shy."

I shook my head, stepping closer to get a better look. "That doesn't make any sense, Ryan." It was a worn and beaten copy of a novel with a small, laminated library barcode on the front. The cover was scratched and dented, and the pages didn't look much better. "*They Never Came Home* by Lois Duncan," I read aloud.

"Creepy," Ryan whispered, wrinkling his nose. He flipped open the first page and jumped back as if it were on fire.

I reached forward, opening it again in an attempt to make sense of what I'd seen. There, on the first page in blood-red smears, were four words that sent chills down my spine.

"What the hell does that mean?" Ryan asked. "Who's Janie?"

I shook my head, unable to speak as the words blurred in my vision. Finally, I found my voice. "I think it means we're in a lot of danger, Ryan. Look at the title—I don't think he plans to let us go home."

I read over the words again, nearly certain they were written in actual blood.

Janie's dead.
You're next.

CHAPTER EIGHT

Grace

I watched as Ryan tossed the book into the garbage can, my heart pounding so loudly in my chest I could hardly hear anything else. He reached for my arm, a light smile on his lips.

"Well, that was a little creepy, huh?"

"Understatement of the year, Ryan. We need to leave!"

"Whoa, wait. What? *Leave*—why? Why would we need to leave?"

I raised a hand in the air in frustration. "Are you kidding me right now? Are we even living the same experience? The man from the woods obviously followed us back here and left that as a warning."

He curled his upper lip in obvious disbelief. "He left a library book as a warning?"

"A library book with a bloody note inside that says Janie's dead and we're next!" Why wasn't he taking this more seriously? It was infuriating.

"Sweetheart, I know you're scared, okay? I get it. But we have no idea why that book was out there. It could've been just under the door frame and, when we came inside earlier, we knocked it to where we could see it."

"That doesn't make any sense!"

"And what does?" he asked, remaining cool and calm as ever. "That the homeless man in the woods brought us a random library book with a note in it to… to what? Scare us? Send us running for the hills?" He ran a hand through his hair casually. "I'm sorry, it just doesn't seem likely."

"The note is obviously a threat. How can you not see that?"

He shook his head. "If anything, it's a prank." There was a pause and he went on. "Look, if he wanted to hurt us, why would he leave us a warning? Why not just knock on the door, and when we open it, he charges in? Or why not try to break in? Leaving us a note makes zero sense to me."

I bit my tongue, trying to think. *Was* I being ridiculous? Was he right? My anxiety often made me think the worst of any given situation, but no, this genuinely felt like underreacting to what was happening. Why couldn't he see that?

"What do you want to do? Do you want to leave? Cancel the honeymoon over *this?*" He pointed toward the garbage, where the book remained, haunting me.

"I don't know," I admitted, feeling frustrated and overwhelmed. "I'm just scared, Ryan."

"You have nothing to be afraid of as long as I'm here. You know that, don't you? I'm right here." He reached for me, pulling me into his arms. I was trembling against him, wanting to say so much more, yet unable to form thoughts that hadn't already been dismissed.

"But what was the shadow? It had to be him."

"You're getting yourself all worked up because you're nervous over our trip and nervous about that man. It's totally understandable. Let's get something for you to drink, and we'll curl up on the couch and watch TV, okay? You just need to breathe for a second, and then you'll realize how ridiculous this all is."

I didn't respond, but he was leading me across the room anyway. He opened the refrigerator, pulling the bottle of moscato out and pouring us each a glass. "Here we go." He spun around, handing mine over. He was acting so normal, I had to wonder why he felt so differently than I did. Didn't he see we were in danger? Did he really believe I was overreacting?

My fingers wrapped around the cool base of the glass, the liquid quivering as my hand shook.

"Come on, sweetheart. Let's not let a few strange happenings affect our entire vacation. I want this to be special for you, okay? I want you to enjoy yourself."

I nodded then, raising the drink to my lips. There was no use arguing. Maybe I *was* being ridiculous.

But the more I thought about it, and the more I ran the night's events over in my head, I didn't think that was the case. Why, then, was my husband so hell-bent on convincing me it was?

CHAPTER NINE

Ryan

The sound of a blaring car alarm jolted me from sleep. I sat up, looking around with blurry vision and a heavy head.

"What is that?" Grace asked from beside me, covering her face with her palm, both eyes still closed.

"It sounds like a car alarm," I said, standing from the bed and stumbling as I tried to unwrap my legs from the covers and hurry toward the window. Because of the shape of the porch and the length of its awning, I couldn't see the car from there, but the closer I grew to the window, the more awake I became, and the more convinced that I was hearing what I thought I was. "Grace," I said, rousing her from sleep as I moved back across the room and pulled on my shorts and a T-shirt. "Get up. Our car alarm is going off."

I didn't want to have to wake her up, not after it had taken me so long to get her calmed down last night, but I had no choice. I tore the door open without waiting to be sure she was awake and hurried through the house. The keys were where I'd left them on the kitchen counter, and I picked them up as I darted past.

I made it out the door, down the steps, and to the driveway before I saw what had happened, my eyes still blurry from sleep. It wasn't possible, yet there it was. The car's windshield had a huge crack in it, a circle that covered most of the glass with small lines like a spider's web splintering off in every direction. In the space where the wipers rested, lay a rock a bit bigger than my fist. I hit the button on the fob in my hand, still processing all I was seeing, and silenced the noise.

Grace was behind me. I heard her hesitant footsteps after the gasp. "What the..." Neither of us seemed to know what to say. I looked around the quiet woods, the birds chirping overhead as if mocking our misfortune. I lifted the rock from its place, staring down at it and then back up at the woods. *Who did this?* It couldn't be, as my wife believed, the man from the woods. It just couldn't. Things like that didn't happen in real life. There had to be a logical explanation. One I could protect her from.

Beside me, Grace looked sick. "Why would anyone do this?" she asked, shaking her head. "It has to be him, Ryan. It has to."

I didn't have an answer for her, but I wanted to hurl the rock at whoever was responsible. I squeezed it tighter, anger bubbling in my chest as I finally came to grips with the truth. It *was* happening. It *had* happened. Now, we had to deal with it.

But I couldn't become obsessed with the homeless man like my wife had. One of us had to keep our wits about us. Everything could be fixed. Explained. But the fact that some random man living in the woods had chosen to torment us just didn't make sense to me.

"We'll have to take it into town to get it fixed," I said, not answering the question she'd posed.

"How much do you think it'll cost?" she asked, blinking back tears. I shook my head. I knew she was thinking that I'd been foolish to engage with the man yesterday. To have given him the money we needed so badly now that we were going to be forced to pay for a repair.

"I don't know, but don't cry. I don't want you to worry about it. We'll get this sorted out."

"But why would he do this?" she asked again through gritted teeth. "We need to go to the police. To hell with getting it fixed. We need help!"

I held up a hand. "Now, hang on, we don't know it was him."

"Why would *anyone* do this, then? And, if it wasn't him, who was it?"

"It may have been an accident," I told her. "Teenagers goofing off in the woods." I didn't, even for a second, believe it. It felt deliberate. I wished the rock held some sort of proof as to who had held it last.

"So, you don't think we should call the police, then? After the noise, the book, and now this?"

The suggestion seemed preposterous. *What would we tell them?* That a rock had hit our windshield? Worse things happened on the interstate all the time. That a book had been left on our porch with some silly painted message? Admitting there was a problem was a problem when we had no idea what was going on. I didn't want to waste the cops' time on unfounded fears, but I could see that she wasn't joking. I gripped her hand, still holding onto the rock.

"I'll tell you what we'll do. We'll take the car into town and see what a mechanic thinks. Hopefully they can get it fixed rather quickly, and we can just move on from it. And then, if anything else happens, we can call the police. But right now, nothing serious has happened. I don't know what the police could do about any of it, honestly."

She frowned, folding her arms across her chest. "They could… I don't know. Could they fingerprint the rock, maybe? Or… I don't know, *something*. Surely."

I looked down at the rock in my hand, dropping it quickly at the thought of them fingerprinting it. Had I messed with the evidence? Tampered with the crime scene? A lump formed in my stomach. "I don't know, Grace. I just don't think going to the police seems smart. I'd rather just have the car fixed and move on. I want to have fun. I want to enjoy this vacation with you, and I really don't like the idea of spending any extra time dealing with this stress than necessary. It was likely just some dumb teenagers in the woods. Insurance should cover the damage, and that'll be the end of it." She swallowed but didn't meet my eye. "Okay?" I pressed.

"So, you really don't think it was him? Am I just being paranoid?"

"You aren't being paranoid. You're just understandably worried. I get it. I know what happened yesterday, meeting that man, freaked you out. And then the noise and the book and this… It's weird timing for sure, but that's all it is, okay? It has to be. You trust me to take care of you, don't you?"

"It was never about not trusting you." She met my gaze then, her expression filled with fear.

"I don't think it was him. Why would he want to damage our property or scare us when we were nice to him? It just"—I offered her a patronizing smile—"honey, it just doesn't make sense." She was so precious when she worried, but I wanted to make sure she felt safe. It had taken me hours to talk her down last night, to convince her that we'd just somehow missed the book before and that the note inside was probably just a joke between whoever had owned it and someone else. It was connected to us in no way.

I almost thought I had her believing it, until now.

"As far as we know, no one else is out here, though. I haven't heard any teenagers, have you? As far as we know, he's the only person for miles."

"Actually, as far as we know, he's not even out here himself anymore," I pointed out.

"But we just saw him yesterday, and then I saw him again from the window. Even if he didn't have anything to do with this or the book, he was definitely around yesterday evening." Her voice raised an octave, and I heard the tears in her tone. By trying not to worry her, I was upsetting her more.

I gave up, sighing and dropping my shoulders finally. "You could be right, I guess. If you really think we should talk to the police, we can."

She nodded before I'd even finished the sentence. "I think they should know someone's been out here and then this happened. And that I saw him outside the house. What if he's dangerous, Ryan? I don't want us to get hurt." Her words sent chills up my arms.

It was ridiculous that someone would be after us. *Wasn't it?* "Okay. We'll see what they say, okay? Maybe they can help put our minds at ease, at least." The corners of her mouth upturned into a small smile. "Everything's going to be okay, I promise."

I wrapped a hand around her shoulder, reaching the other up to brush a piece of hair from her eyes. When I did, I froze. "What the…"

I lowered my palm, both of us staring at it in shock. My hand was streaked with navy blue, as if I'd been playing with markers. I looked at the other one, but it was clean. On the ground, the rock lay, and I bent down and lifted it to get a closer look then dropped it again, true, ice-cold panic tearing through me for the first time.

It was too late. Even if I'd wanted to hide it from her, to protect her, I knew she'd seen it already. Tears filled her eyes again. "Ryan…"

"It's okay. It's going to be okay." My body was ice cold with fear and adrenaline, and I wanted nothing more than to get the paint off my hands. I had to stay calm. I couldn't let her see me upset. She deserved better.

I stared down at the rock again as I ushered her inside. From where it lay, I could see a faint hint of the blue paint on its side.

The blue letters.

The warning.

One little painted word that sent alarm and confusion ricocheting through me.

Run.

CHAPTER TEN

Grace

We drove the winding roads on our way into town in total silence. Ryan gripped the steering wheel until his knuckles were pure white while struggling to see beyond the smashed windshield. I clasped my fingers into tight fists, too worked up to speak.

We'd called the insurance company when we finally reached a point, several miles up the road from the cabin, where we had cellular service. They gave us the number and address for the closest mechanic's shop, but it was at my insistence that Ryan had finally agreed we'd go to the police first.

The trees surrounding the unpaved roads were peaceful and serene, still as beautiful as I'd remembered from the drive in, yet now they carried an ominous tone. What secrets did these woods hold? What dangers were lurking?

"Shit," Ryan said under his breath, and I felt the car lurch as he took a foot off the gas, his brows lowered. I followed his gaze to the rearview mirror, then checked the one to my side. Flashing blue and red lights reflected back at me. We were going to the police, but as luck would have it, they'd come to us. He slowed the vehicle even more, pulling it to the side of the gravel road quickly.

I watched the police cruiser slow down, coming to a stop behind us. The lights continued flashing, and we sat in complete, tension-filled silence. After a few moments, Ryan said, "Get the registration out of the glove box, will you?"

I nodded, retrieving the envelope with our insurance and registration information before passing it across the car. He opened it, pulling the papers out and laying them across the dashboard as he opened his wallet and produced his identification.

I looked at my mirror again, seeing the driver's door of the cruiser open and a man step out. He was tall and thin with a thick mustache and dark sunglasses. When he made it to Ryan's window, he leaned down, lifting his glasses to reveal dark, unreadable eyes.

"You've got quite the crack in the ole windshield there, don't ya?"

"Yes, sir," Ryan said, exhaustion in his tone. "We had a rock thrown at our windshield."

The man paused, looking at us both strangely. "That's unfortunate. I need to see your license and registration, please."

Ryan handed over the documents, and the man looked over them carefully. After what seemed like an eternity of waiting, he handed them back. "Where are you folks headed?"

"Just into the town right up here," Ryan said. "Dukeville, I think it's called. To report this to the local police—I'm not sure if that would be you?—and then we need to see if we can get the windshield fixed quickly, before we're scheduled to head home on Saturday."

The officer nodded. "Yeah, that'd be Dukeville, and I'm the sheriff." He stretched out his hand, and Ryan shook it. "Sheriff Ritter. You're in town visiting?"

"We're staying in a cabin just a few miles down the road."

"Well, I'm sorry to have pulled you over, but I can't have you driving all over my streets with damage like this." He rapped his knuckles against the windshield. "It's too dangerous for you and for my citizens. Ordinarily, I'd have to give you a ticket for driving like this. But"—he tucked one hand in his pocket, inhaling deeply—"seeing as how it's a nice day out and you're visiting, I guess I can let it slide if you'll go straight to the shop and promise me you won't drive the car again until it's fixed."

Ryan looked at me, his lips drawn tight in contemplation. Finally, he nodded, then looked at the sheriff. "Thank you, yeah. We really appreciate that."

"It's no problem, but we do need to get you to a mechanic right away. There's one here in town, Elliot's. He'll get you fixed up and on your way in no time flat. If you need to report what happened, I'm happy to meet with you down at the station after we've gotten that squared away."

He looked up ahead. "We really should have you towed the rest of the way into town, but it'll take a few hours to get someone out here. I'll tell you what… I'll drive in front with my lights flashing, and lead you to the shop. You can follow me, okay? That way we make sure you make it safely, and you aren't endangering other drivers on the road."

We hadn't passed a single other driver since we'd left the cabin that morning, but I wasn't about to say that.

"Thank you, Sheriff," Ryan said. "We can't thank you enough for helping us out."

The man nodded. "You betcha. Give me just a minute to get going, and then stay close." With that, he walked away and Ryan shifted the car into gear as we waited for him to pull around us, lights on, and lead us into town.

About fifteen minutes later, when we finally arrived in Dukeville, I was still a ball of nerves. Finally, though, we pulled into a small parking lot for the mechanic's shop. The garage was a large, white barn that sat back from the road, a gravel lot on each side and in the front filled with cars, tires, and car parts. Black letters had been hand painted across the front: Elliot's Garage.

As we slowed the car to a stop next to the police cruiser, a short, plump man with overalls and thick glasses walked out of the open door of the garage. His bottom lip was swollen with chewing tobacco. When we stepped from the car, he hawked brown spit onto the ground. I watched with disgust as the dark brown saliva painted the gray of the rocks. The sheriff gave a wave to the man but made no move to get out of his car.

"Can I help you folks?" the mechanic asked, speaking louder than necessary as we grew nearer. "What's going on?" His stubby, grease-stained finger outstretched toward the police cruiser, then toward us.

"Yeah, we're hoping you can. We need to get our windshield replaced," Ryan said, reaching out his hand to shake the man's.

"Don't think you'll want to shake mine," he said with a chuckle, staring at his greasy palms.

Ryan withdrew his arm, realizing his mistake but hardly missing a beat. "We're hoping to have it fixed before Saturday, though. Any chance that's possible?"

"You got your insurance information, or are you paying in cash?"

Ryan reached into his back pocket, pulling out his worn, leather wallet and producing the insurance card he'd shoved in there after being pulled over. "Here you go. Do you have any idea how long it might take? Or how much it might cost?"

The man grunted, looking over to the car. "My glass guy comes on Tuesdays."

"Okay, so… That's today. Is he going to be able to fix it today?"

"I'd have to see," he said nonchalantly. "I've got another car in front of ya."

"Okay, great," Ryan said, not missing a beat. "That would be amazing. We're scheduled to head out Saturday morning. It'll be done by then, you think? I hate to rush you. It's just that we're not from around here, and the sheriff says we have to get it fixed before we can drive it again or else he'll give us a ticket. I'm taking my wife on a nice honeymoon that was out of our budget anyway, so we really can't afford a windshield repair *and* a ticket, you know?"

The man looked him up and down at the 'not from around here' comment, as if to say that was obvious. "Yep, I'll see what I can do."

I looked behind me, spying the sheriff still sitting next to our car, watching us. I knew he was doing something nice by not ticketing us, but didn't he see what a predicament we were in? This was a nightmare. What were we supposed to do if he couldn't fix the car? We certainly couldn't wait around until next Tuesday, and the man didn't seem to hear or care about the urgency in Ryan's tone.

"Okay…" Ryan said, his voice breathy. "Okay, so what do you need from me to get started?"

The man gestured toward the card. "Let's go into the office, get a copy of that, and take some of your information."

As we started to walk off, the sheriff's car finally pulled out of the lot. We followed the man back into the barn and to the right through a closed, metal door. The stale-smelling office was small and cluttered; a cheerful-looking woman with bright red lipstick and oversized, black-framed glasses on her button nose smiled up at us. She put down the iced tea in her hand and stood, touting a round, pregnant belly I hadn't noticed when she was sitting.

"Andrea, can you make a copy of these folks' insurance card and get his information for a windshield replacement?"

"Of course, hi! Come in." She gestured toward the dusty chairs in front of her desk, though they were both filled with brown cardboard boxes. "Just move those right out of your way."

We did as we were told and took a seat. Once we were seated, she followed suit, sitting back in her chair, and the man turned and walked out of the room without a word. "Okay, so he said you need a windshield replaced, right? Let's get that paperwork going for you. Do you have your insurance card with you?"

Ryan handed her the card he'd been holding for what seemed like a long time, and she turned around in her chair, making a copy on the large and noisy copy machine behind her. She handed the card back to Ryan and smiled at me warmly. "I haven't seen you two around here before. Are you new in town or just passing through?"

"We're staying in a cabin not far from here. This was the closest town."

Her expression warmed even more. "Oh, that's nice. Yeah, we have so many cute little cabins around here. It's such a nice, peaceful area for them, too. Not too far from most of the attractions, but far enough out you get a little space to yourself, right? Just a sweet little getaway. That's great. Well, we thank you for coming in. We always appreciate new business."

"Yeah, we're enjoying the area," Ryan said.

I spoke up. "I hate to be abrupt, but do you think you'll be able to get the car fixed today? Or at least this week? The man mentioned that your glass guy comes on Tuesdays, but he said there's someone ahead of us for repairs. I don't mean to sound like I'm trying to cut in line, but we are scheduled to leave and head back home on Saturday before eleven, and I'm not really sure what we'll do if the car is still not fixed. We live several hours away, so it wouldn't really work for us to come back for it…"

I trailed off, unsure of what I was trying to say. Maybe I sounded insensitive, but my stress level was incredibly high, and I was exhausted from pretending everything was fine.

"I understand how stressful it can be," she said softly.

I nodded. "Yes. I'm sorry. I guess I'm just trying to ask what you think our best option is, so we can start to make arrangements either way."

The woman smiled, and I noticed a splash of red lipstick on her front tooth. "No need to apologize, sweetie. I totally understand. The man who does our glass repair, Tony, is usually good about getting in whatever we need from him during the week"—she nodded as she spoke—"unless he has something else scheduled and can only be here for a specific time. I can contact him before he gets here to check on his schedule, and then, if he can't get you finished today, I'll get him back by the end of the week so we're sure you two can head home on Saturday as planned. Would that be okay?" She picked up a pencil. "You said Saturday before eleven, right?"

"Yes, that's right. But preferably sooner."

"Oh, yes, of course." She jotted it down, underlining it twice. "I have to write everything down these days. 'Mommy brain,' as they say." She giggled.

I let out a sigh of relief. "Thank you so much."

She waved off the thanks, grinning broadly. "Oh, please. It's my pleasure. You *can* thank us by sending your friends our way if they're ever in the area, though."

"We certainly will," Ryan said.

"We'll just plan to call you when we've heard back from your insurance to give you an update, and then again when it's ready for pick up. What's a good phone number for you?"

Ryan recited it, but I interrupted him at the end. "We don't have service where we're staying, though, so the call wouldn't go through. Maybe we could just plan to drive down to a place where we have service and call and check in tomorrow and then again on Friday, if it's not done sooner. To make sure things are in order?"

"Oh, right!" She clicked her tongue, tapping her chin with her finger. "That does make things a bit more complicated, doesn't it? Yeah, I think that would work fine." She slid a business card across the desk, and Ryan took it, though we already had their phone number. "But how are you going to be able to drive? Do you have someone who can get you home and back?"

"No, we're going to have to rent a car," Ryan answered.

She looked unsure. "Well, I hate to say it, but I'm afraid you're going to have a hard time finding a taxi *or* a car rental place around here. Most folks know someone who can get them around. Anyway, you're more than welcome to wait here while you try to figure something out."

Ryan looked at me, and I knew he felt the same panic I did. What were we going to do? Seeming to sense the tension, the woman stood up.

"I'll give you two a minute to talk while I step outside and take a few pictures of the damage for the insurance claim. It won't be any trouble at all to have someone drop you off at your place if you need us to. We can even arrange to have it dropped off when it's done. Of course, that does leave you stranded at the cabin with no way to get to town if you needed to, so I understand if that's not a viable option. Just talk about it. I'll be right back."

With that, she disappeared from the room, cell phone in hand, and left us alone. "What kind of town doesn't have taxis?" Ryan asked with a defined scowl.

"What are we going to do? We still need to go talk to the sheriff at the station after we leave here."

He shook his head. "That's not really a priority right now, Grace. I mean, I think we have bigger issues. The sheriff didn't seem too concerned when we told him what had happened and the insurance said they'll likely cover the damage, anyway. I don't think we need to go to the police, or that it'll even be an option at this point."

He pulled out his phone, scrolling through an internet search I couldn't see. "Let me call around and find out what we can do."

My heart sank, but I didn't dare argue. It was no use.

Ten minutes later, Andrea returned. "Not good news, I'm guessing?" she asked, reading our grim expressions.

"We can't find anyone who can deliver a car anywhere close to here. I mean, what do people here do when something like this happens?"

"It's a small town," she said sympathetically. "We call our neighbors, our friends. We don't have the resources the big cities do, but we have a whole lotta heart." She pressed her palm to her chest. "I don't want you folks to worry, okay? I'll call the sheriff and see if he can arrange for someone to give you a lift back home. Then, as soon as it's fixed, we'll get the car delivered to you. How does that sound?"

"I don't know…" Ryan said after a moment of silence. "I don't like the idea of being all the way out there without a car."

She pursed her lips. "Oh. I hate the idea that your trip will get cancelled because of this. What if I can get Tony to agree to fixing the windshield today? Then we can bring it back to you either this evening or first thing in the morning. Would that make you feel better?"

Ryan looked at me, and I chewed my lip. "I don't know. We still don't know who did this. What if it was someone who meant to do us harm, and we're stuck out there without a car?"

The woman sucked in a sharp breath. "You think someone did this on purpose?"

"No—" Ryan said.

At the same time, I said, "Maybe—" We paused, and he looked at me, nodding. I went on. "We don't know for sure, but I have a suspicion. The rock that hit our windshield was painted with what looked like the word *run*—"

"We don't know for sure that's what it said. We don't even know if it *said* anything. It was smeared from me holding it," Ryan added.

I went on, ignoring him. "And we met a man in the woods yesterday. We think he was homeless, but we don't know for sure. I could swear I saw him watching our cabin afterward. From the woods. And then there was this really creepy book left on our porch…"

"Oh my…" she squeaked. "That *is* concerning. I can see why you wouldn't want to be out there without a car. Have you called the police?"

"That's where we were heading this morning when we were pulled over by Sheriff Ritter. He said we needed to come here and get the car fixed so he didn't have to give us a ticket. He actually led us here to make sure we made it okay. We were planning to go talk to him at the station after this," Ryan said. "But without a car…"

She glanced out the window. "That explains why I thought I saw him pulling in earlier. Well, here, why don't I call Sheriff Ritter and see if he can stop back by? Then you can report what happened and get a ride back home all at once. I'd say he's probably stopped in to the cafe up the street for his mid-morning coffee. It shouldn't take him any time to get back here."

"I'd hate to put him out having to drive us back to the cabin," Ryan said under his breath, his neck flaming scarlet. He hated having to ask for help.

Andrea locked eyes with me, obviously concerned for our safety. What other options did we have? I couldn't see any. He always wanted to fix things himself, refusing to ask for help. Perhaps it was a man thing, that he was afraid to show any signs of weakness, but it was absolutely infuriating.

"Oh, nonsense. It'll give him something to do. A town this slow, and he's bound to get bored." She was already dialing on her phone. "You two just sit tight. You can tell him your concerns, and then, if you want to go ahead with the vacation, I'll see if he can take you back to your cabin afterward, too. Two birds, one stone." She winked and sauntered out of the room, leaving us to sit in silence alone.

Ryan looked like he still wanted to object, but he didn't say a word.

"Are you mad at me?" I asked, keeping my voice low.

He looked shocked, moving his hand to my lap and squeezing my thigh. "Of course not. Why would you ask that?"

"I know you weren't sure about going to the police in the first place. I don't want to feel like I'm forcing you, I just really think we should at least see what they think about it all."

He huffed air from his nose, his mouth drawing in on one side. "I know. You're probably right. I'm just always worried about wasting his time with something silly."

"It's his job, Ryan. And it could be our lives."

His smile was patronizing, and I could tell he thought I was being overdramatic, but he didn't argue. Instead, he said, "We'll see what he has to say." I nodded, unable to talk about it anymore without getting angrier, so we spent the rest of our wait in total silence.

After a few minutes of silence, the door reopened and Sheriff Ritter reappeared with a red paper cup of coffee, Andrea just steps behind him. He smiled at us warmly, though there was still a reserved nature to him I had noticed right away. We were outsiders. He didn't trust us.

"Hello. Nice to see you folks again. Andrea tells me you've had some sort of run in with a"—he cleared his throat and glanced at her—"man in the woods? And that you think it might be connected to your busted windshield?"

Ryan adjusted in his seat. "Yes, sir." He stood to face the sheriff. "You see, we went for a hike in the woods near our cabin and there was this… well, like you said, a man in the woods. He had a tent, a few basic items… We assumed he was homeless, so I gave him a few of our supplies, food, and a straw that filters water so he could get something to drink."

Ryan cleared his throat, swiping his hands across his pants. "When we got home, my wife thought she saw him in the woods outside our cabin, but we couldn't be sure. But later that night, we heard noises outside our cabin, and my wife thought she saw a shadow outside the door. We thought it might be a bear, but we found a book on the porch. Now, it might've already been there and we just somehow missed it. It was small and dark and almost blended in with the welcome mat, but there was a note inside of it that said…"

He looked my way. "What was it? *Janie*… I think? 'Janie died and you're next,' or something like that. Then, this morning, a rock was thrown at our windshield… Well, you saw what happened there. There was blue paint on the rock that looked like it said 'run,' but we couldn't be sure."

For someone who had thought I was crazy five minutes ago, he seemed to be all too eager to lay out the events as they'd happened.

The sheriff nodded, taking a sip of his coffee. He wasn't taking notes or anything. Was that normal? "Well, that does sound like you've had your fair share of hijinks. We do have a few members of the homeless population nearby that have taken shelter in the woods around town. Generally, they've been peaceful, though." He looked at Andrea again. "We haven't had any reports of them causing any problems." She shook her head in agreement. "Where are you staying exactly?"

"We're in a cabin off Dolly's Drive and Overlook Lane," Ryan said. "Way back off the road. Really secluded."

The sheriff looked at Andrea, both of their faces fading a few degrees paler. "Two thirty-one?" he asked. That was the house number.

We nodded in unison. "Do you know it?" Ryan asked.

He pressed his lips together in confirmation. "Unfortunately, I do. And that explains what's happened. I'm assuming you know the history of the murder cabin?"

"*Murder* cabin?" Ryan asked, his words sending chills over my arms.

"If you guys had told me that was where you were staying, I could've told you that was probably what was going on," Andrea said.

I shook my head. "What are you talking about?" Ryan looked at me with confusion.

"You do know the history of the cabin where you're staying, don't you?" Sheriff Ritter asked.

"No," we said in unison.

He sighed heavily, looking behind him to where a stack of boxes sat in the chair against the far wall. He moved them from the seat and sat down, gesturing for Ryan to do the same. When he had, the sheriff began to tell his story, his face solemn.

"I hate to be the one to tell you, but the cabin where you're staying has a very grim history. Two separate murders have occurred there, and we've yet to catch the person responsible." At seeing the shock on our faces, he leaned forward, trying to be reassuring.

"Now, I don't want you to worry too much. The murders happened years ago. Nothing violent has happened there in a long time, but we do have our fair share of lurkers. Lots of… what do they call 'em, *scary tourists*?"

"Dark tourists," Andrea corrected him.

I'd heard of that. Ryan and I had seen a Netflix documentary about them recently.

The sheriff grimaced. "Right, dark tourists. They rent out the cabin, see how long they can make it. Most don't end up lasting. Unfortunately, some local teenagers have taken to using the woods nearby to get drunk. It's something we've been monitoring for quite a while, but they've never done anything violent. I'd say things got a little out of hand last night, and I am sorry for that." He paused.

"That explains why the book was from a school library," Ryan said, looking at me. "It was just a bunch of kids, like I said."

The sheriff nodded. "I'm sorry they did that to you. Most folks around here are friendly, but as I said… teenagers give us all a run for our money now and again. I am sorry and, frankly, rather surprised you didn't know about the history of the cabin, though. I expected it would be harder to find a listing for it online that didn't include the history."

He ran a hand over his forehead, groaning. "The owner capitalizes on it, as you can imagine. Calls it by that name, the *murder cabin,* in most postings, though I've asked him to stop."

I wrapped my arms around myself, trying to rub away the goosebumps on my arms. "So, do you think we're in danger? Should we head home now instead of waiting?"

The sheriff leaned back in his chair, looking hesitant to answer. "Oh, no. I wouldn't say that. I… I don't know that it's necessary for you to leave. I can have a patrol car monitor the area for teens and the man you said you saw. Most likely, though, it's just a one-off. Like I said, nothing violent has happened there in years. But we aren't immune to our fair share of pranks and rowdy teenagers. Especially as the fall gets here and we get closer to Halloween." He rolled his eyes. "That's when all the nutters come out, isn't it?"

I swallowed without response, not feeling reassured. Ryan reached for my hand, squeezing it gently. "Well, we'd appreciate you checking it out for us, Sheriff. If for nothing else than our peace of mind."

"I'm happy to. Andrea mentioned you need a ride out there? I can check out the area while I'm there, see if I see signs of anything or anyone suspicious, and then I'll send someone again at dusk to be sure the area remains clear. And we'll get your car delivered first thing in the morning to get you folks all squared away."

He patted his knee dramatically. "I'm sorry your welcome to our town has been anything less than friendly, but hopefully we can get that fixed for you right now."

He smiled, standing finally, and tipping his head toward us without waiting for a response. "I'll wait outside by my car so you all can finish up, okay?"

"Thank you, sir," Ryan said before looking at me. There was concern in his expression, though he was obviously trying to hide it.

When the sheriff walked from the room, Ryan swallowed, breaking eye contact with me to look at Andrea again. "Well, that was unexpected." His laugh was uneasy.

"Do you remember what happened?" I asked her. "The murders, I mean."

"Oh, it was big news for a while," she said, rubbing her stomach rhythmically. "The cabin's been a rental property for years, as long as I've been alive, at least. But this all happened about twenty years ago. One girl, she was younger, I think… they found her body when guests arrived. She was… er, well, they'd *tried* to bury her in the yard, but they hadn't done a good job. And then it rained…"

Andrea shivered, and I felt my throat tightening at her description. "They didn't find any other bodies on the property when they excavated it, and I don't remember them even having any suspects, honestly. The next one wasn't long after… She was an older woman." She sighed dramatically, batting her eyelashes. "Well, probably close to my age now, but she seemed old at the time. I don't remember as much about that one, but I know she was found in the house."

Her eyes were haunted as she stared into space. She blinked out of a trance, smiling at us stiffly. "Like the sheriff said, it was a long time ago. I'm sure there's nothing to worry about now," she said.

But, in fact, she didn't seem sure at all. I knew then none of us were sure of anything. The chances of there being nothing to worry about were very slim.

CHAPTER ELEVEN

Ryan

The ride back to the cabin was filled with Sheriff Ritter telling us all about the history of the town, how his family had come there over a century before and never left. He talked very little about the cabin, much to my relief. His insistence that we would be fine, that the killer was long gone, that we were just the victims of a prank last night, and this area was extremely safe under normal circumstances came only at the end of the ride, as we neared the long, secluded driveway I'd been excited to enter not so long ago. It seemed like a lifetime had passed since then.

"Anyway," he said, as we pulled into the drive. He looked at us in the rearview mirror of his cruiser, the bars between us from the backseat obstructing my view only slightly. "My point is, I've always thought it was a serial killer that stopped off in our area for a while. The murders happened less than three years apart. Both women. And nothing since. I think he made his way into our area for the time, for whatever reason, but has since left. I wouldn't be bringing you back, wouldn't allow the place to still be rented out, if I didn't believe you were perfectly safe."

"Thank you," I said for what felt like the hundredth time. I just wished he'd stop talking. "And thank you, again, for the ride."

"It was my pleasure," he said, pulling the car to a stop in front of the cabin. He turned off the engine and stepped from the car, opening my door so we could slide out. Grace hadn't let go of my arm the whole ride. "I'll take a walk around, make sure everything looks normal, and alert you if anything doesn't." He looked toward the woods. "If you need anything, you just call, okay?" He slid a business card from his pocket. I realized quickly it was a business card from a local Mexican restaurant. The sheriff flipped it over and rested it against his car, jotting down a phone number and handing it to me. He slid his pen back into his pocket and looked at me. "You take care now, you hear?"

A shiver ran across my skin as I nodded, and I felt Grace grip onto me tighter. I rubbed her hand before pointing to the painted-blue rock on the ground. "Oh, before you go, there's the rock that was thrown at the windshield. If you need to take it in for… I don't know, fingerprints or something."

The sheriff smiled at me, making me feel stupid, but made no move to pick up the rock. "Thanks. I'll keep that in mind." With that, he turned toward the woods. "I'd better get going and let you get back to your day." We watched as he disappeared into the edge of the woods surrounding our cabin, obviously not fearful in any sense of the word.

I pulled Grace toward the cabin, jabbed my fingers into the keypad to enter the code, and hurried us both inside. Once we were in, I turned the deadbolt quickly, heaving a breath. "This stays locked," I warned her, though she obviously didn't need to be told. She fell into my arms, her body shaking with sudden sobs, as if she were a dam that had suddenly burst. I wouldn't let myself get upset. I needed to be strong for her. "It's going to be okay. I promise you it will. I won't let anything happen to you."

When she pulled away, dabbing her wet eyes, she shook her head. "I don't understand. How did you not know about this place? The listing didn't mention anything about its past?"

I shook my head, feeling like I'd been duped. Normally, when I booked a place, I spent time checking it out on Google and social media to see if I could find any pictures, posts, or crime reports for the area that weren't on the owner's site. I knew well enough to know how easy it was to hide the bad reviews. This time, though, I'd trusted Everleigh's advice when she'd told me this place would be perfect. I didn't want to spend too long looking into it and risk missing out on such a great deal. "I don't think so. There were good reviews and the pictures were beautiful—the price couldn't have been better."

"Well, now we know why." She scoffed.

"Everleigh sent me this listing. She told me you'd like the privacy and seclusion of it. I was just trying to do something nice for you by taking your needs into consideration. I had no idea about the history. I'm so sorry, Grace. I was trying to find somewhere to ease your anxiety and…"

"And you booked us a murder cabin," she said, her face solemn for a moment before a slight smile played at the corner of her lips. "Oh my god, I'm going to kill her. Wait until she hears how bad her suggestion was." She laughed. "I'll bet she has no idea what she's done."

I laughed then, too, unsure why we were laughing, but it felt good to get the stress out somehow.

"Why did you ask her anyway?" she asked when her laughter had calmed down.

"I didn't," I said. "She sent me an email with a link to this place and said that you had mentioned we were planning to go away on a vacation and had asked her to keep Stanley. She said she thought this cabin was perfect for you if we hadn't already booked a place. I hadn't, and I agreed with her that it was exactly what you needed. I couldn't find anything nearly this secluded and nice for the price. I couldn't believe it still had availability."

"No surprise there." She rubbed her temple. "Perfect, hm? Well, she hit the nail on the head there, didn't she?" She laughed again. "Wait until I tell her…" She chewed her lip nervously, shaking her head.

"Are you okay?"

She nodded then shook her head. "I'm trying to be."

I glanced out the windows across the room, overlooking the tops of the trees. "We can leave if you want."

"We literally can't," she pointed out.

"I mean by tomorrow. Andrea said we'll get the car back either this evening or tomorrow morning. We can leave as soon as we have it."

"Would it be ruining the honeymoon for you?" Tears brimmed her eyes again.

"*No,*" I said quickly. "No, of course not. Honey, I don't care where we are or what we're doing. As long as I'm with you, I'm good." I kissed her head, then her forehead and her nose, working my way down to her lips. Her cool tears brushed my cheek, and I felt her arms wrap around my neck as she fell deeper into my kiss.

I cupped her face, unable to hide my smile, despite our locked lips. Warmth spread throughout my body in a way only her touch could make happen. I ran my fingers through her hair, pressing my body against hers as I felt myself hardening with excitement.

She let out a soft sigh, and I lowered my hands to her waist, scooping her up to rest on the counter. Her legs wrapped around my waist, and I lifted her shirt over her head, running my kisses along her collarbone and in between her breasts. The adrenaline of the moment before was rushing from our bodies, and I felt myself filling with excitement and desire.

I wanted her. Needed her. Nothing had ever been clearer. I tore off her bra next, pressing my face to her chest and inhaling her scent. She tossed her head back, releasing a louder sigh as my tongue met her nipple. I grabbed her then, scooping her from the counter and rushing across the room, my mouth back on hers as we fumbled our way toward the bedroom. I couldn't wait any longer. I wanted her to know I'd take care of her in every way for the rest of our lives, and this was my favorite way to prove it.

*

When we had finished, we lay together—a tangled mess in the sheets, our legs still intertwined. Her fingers ran through my hair, her scent still on my lips. I could've lain there all day.

"I do want to go home," she whispered, her voice soft, almost like a dream. I hadn't realized I'd been falling asleep until that moment.

My eyes opened after a moment. "Did you say something?" *Had* it been a dream?

"I do want to go home, Ryan," she whispered again, still playing with my hair.

I ran a hand across her bare stomach. "Then home we shall go."

"I'm sorry this isn't what you had planned."

"Me too," I admitted. "But I'd rather us be safe than worry about that. We can take a second, *even later* honeymoon another time." I laughed, trying to get her to join in.

"I love you for always protecting me."

Her words sent new heat through my body—pride. It was all I wanted. To protect her. To care for her. To love her. "I always will," I swore. A vow. Like the ones we'd made just six months before. God, I loved her so much it almost hurt.

"Stanley will be glad to see us," she said.

"I'll have to go back to sharing you with him." The smile faded from my face, though she couldn't see it with my head resting on her chest.

"Well, you still have me all to yourself for one more night." Her hands slowed in my hair, the movements suddenly sensual in an inexplicable way.

"I plan to take advantage of that," I said with a deep chuckle, running a finger around her belly button.

"Oh, you do, do you?"

"Mhm." I kissed the top of her breast. "At least a few times."

"I look forward to it." She laughed again. I loved her carefree giggle, though I felt like I rarely heard it. It seemed like all too often, she was guarded and cautious, but I lived for the moments when she let that guard down with me. Moments where she was happy and protected. Like now. I felt pride swell in my chest at the realization I'd done that. I'd taken her fears away. I'd made her happy. "Ryan?" her voice was soft again, but filled with concern this time.

"Hm?" I looked up at her, my brows furrowed.

"Why didn't you want to go to the police?"

I swallowed, my body suddenly cold. I couldn't tell her. She could never know the truth. I looked out the window, where the sun had crossed over the house and was shining through our window with a blinding brightness. I sat up, staring down at her.

"What do you mean?"

"It seemed like you didn't want to talk to the police about the car… Is there a reason?" There was something in her eyes I couldn't quite put my finger on. What did she know? Not *it*, obviously. She couldn't know that. No one did. But something…

"I just didn't want to waste their time, I guess. Like I told you." I scratched the back of my head before reaching for my pants on the floor. I stood up, pulling them on as I looked over her exposed body. If it were up to me, she'd stay like that all day. But I needed the distraction of putting on clothes. I needed to steer the conversation from where it was. "You hungry?"

She sat up slowly, stretching her arms up above her head before grabbing her shirt from the edge of the bed. She pulled it over her head, no bra on, and then reached for her underwear and shorts. She stood and pulled them on without answering, and I walked out of the room toward the kitchen, though I desperately didn't want to leave her.

"Are you avoiding the subject?" she asked after I'd opened the cabinet and pulled down two wine glasses.

"Hm?" I turned to face her, glasses in hand.

"You know you can tell me anything," she said, her voice hesitant. "We shouldn't have secrets between us."

I removed the wine bottle from the refrigerator and poured myself a glass, despite it being just barely lunchtime. If we were going to have this conversation, I needed alcohol. And vast quantities of it at that.

"What are you talking about? We don't have secrets."

"Then why won't you tell me why you were so hesitant to go to the police?"

"Because I didn't want to look stupid if it was nothing," I said. I glanced out the window, toward the empty drive. "Which, I'm guessing is the case, because the sheriff's car is gone."

"What?" she squeaked, rushing toward the door to look outside. "He can't have already checked the entire woods surrounding the cabin. There hasn't been enough time."

"I'm sure he checked enough," I said, flooded with relief as I took another sip of my wine. Thank God we were moving on to something else.

"That right there," Grace said, shutting the door. When I turned around, she was wagging her finger at me, her face flushed red with anger. "Why aren't you more worried? We're standing in a room where people were literally murdered." She looked down, and I had the vague suspicion she was wondering where it had happened. "I know I worry more than you, but you should still be concerned."

"I *am* concerned," I told her. "Of course, I am. But the sheriff said it was nothing, and I trust him. He checked the woods and left, obviously finding nothing. I think we're fine. I agree, I don't want to stay here any longer than we have to, knowing what we know. I'm going to be emailing the owner and asking for a refund. He should've been required to disclose this before we booked it. Either way, though, we're going to leave as soon as we can. But there's literally nothing else we can do, and worrying about it won't change that." I held out her wine glass to her, and she took it hesitantly. "One of us has to be calm here. I'm just trying to be reasonable."

"And I'm not?" she demanded, her voice quivering with rage.

"That's not what I mean, sweetheart." She was upset, and rightfully so. Why had I said that? "I just know how stressed out you can get, and I'm trying to lighten that load."

"You always do that, Ryan. You always act like I'm so fragile and you have to be this big, strong man. Can you not just be real with me? Are you or are you not afraid?"

"I mean, *afraid* seems a bit strong of a word. *Concerned*, sure. But I believe that it could've been teenagers, like the sheriff said. I mean, you're the one who wanted to go to the police and see what they thought. And we did that. We told him everything, and he said we were fine. That it was just stupid kids playing a prank that went wrong, which is what I'd said originally. We have no reason to think differently. Why are you pushing so hard for it to be something else?"

"Even if he's right, even if it's just 'dumb kids,' what if it's a window to the cabin they throw rocks at next? What if they try to break in?"

"They're *teenagers,* Grace. Not criminal masterminds. They were probably just goofing off and made a mistake. And you heard the sheriff say he's going to send someone out to check the woods at dusk to ward them off in case they come back. We'll leave the porch light on, too. That way they think we're still awake. That would've been the smart thing to do last night. There's just no reason to let yourself get all worked up over nothing."

"But that's just it. They didn't *just* come around dusk, Ryan. With the book, sure, fine. But they had to have come this morning. We didn't sleep through the car alarm all night last night. You honestly think a group of teenagers was partying around the cabin at six in the morning?"

I swallowed, thinking. "I don't know what to think. And it's obvious we disagree, but I don't want to fight with you, babe. I just want to get through the night and get home. I know you're scared, but I promise I won't let anything happen to you."

"That's an empty promise, Ryan. You can't promise you won't let anything happen to me, and you know it. Anything could happen. A bomb could blow up. A shooter could come. A bear could break in."

I couldn't help the snicker that I tried to suppress at the outlandish suggestions, but her eyes widened, and I knew it was the wrong thing to do. She was incredibly serious, and I was being insensitive. I hated myself for it.

"I'm sorry. I'm not laughing at you. You're right. I know you're right. What I should've said is that I will do everything in my power to protect you from anything that might happen. First thing in the morning, or as soon as they return our car, we'll get out of here. Never have to think of this place again." Her shoulders fell, and I couldn't tell if it was disappointment or relief dragging them down. "I love you. I just don't want to fight," I said.

She nodded but didn't respond.

"Do you love me, too?"

She furrowed her brow. "You know I do."

I reached for her, drawing her to me as she sulked. I put one hand on her waist, the other on my wine glass, pretending to dance in the small space of the kitchen. To my great relief, she rested her head on my shoulder, the fight seemingly over.

"I don't know what I'd ever do without you," I whispered, resting my cheek on her head.

"Let's hope we don't ever have to find out," she replied.

"Never. I won't let it happen." She smiled, but I felt the sheer terror in my chest rising at the thought, the truth in my words not resonating with her. I would *sooner die* than let it happen, and I wanted her to know that. But this moment wasn't the time for my intensity, so I swallowed the confession down, lulling myself to tranquility as the thought of everything I wanted to say repeated in my head.

We will never be apart.

I won't let it happen.

Couldn't.

I'd sooner die.

Oh, Grace, you don't know what you mean to me.

I had no idea how wrong I was.

CHAPTER TWELVE

Grace

Five hours later, we were several glasses of wine in, curled together on the couch with a sitcom on the TV. I needed the laughter, though I'd basically checked out from listening. Instead, I spent the evening watching every bit of movement out the window, listening for every noise. The glasses of wine had helped to loosen me up a bit, but still, my anxiety was at an all-time high.

On top of worrying about the house, about the man in the woods, and about the car, I was also trying to figure out how to bring up what I so desperately needed to. The thing I'd been unable to since we started dating, since we got engaged, and since we got married. He needed to know the truth, but I couldn't bring myself to say it.

What does it change, really?

What will it matter?

For me, nothing. But, for him, perhaps everything. He'd sworn just hours ago to never let anything break us apart, to not know what he'd do without me, but was that the truth? How could he swear it when he didn't have all the facts? When he didn't know what he was swearing.

"What are you thinking about?" he asked, interrupting my thoughts.

The truth? What I was always thinking about this time of night. The thing that haunted me.

My answer? "Nothing really… What about you?"

He smiled, his attention turned completely to me then. "You seem distracted tonight. Just because of all that's going on, or something else?"

"I'm not distracted," I promised. But, of course, I was.

He didn't respond right away, though his eyes said he knew something was wrong. I sighed, asking the question I had earlier. Hoping it would lead where I needed it to go now.

"You're right. I am a little distracted. I just keep thinking about earlier. I know you said there wasn't a reason why you didn't want to go to the police, and that you just didn't want to bother them if it was nothing, but are you sure there wasn't any other reason? I just feel like you aren't telling me everything."

"What else would there be to tell? I don't understand what you're saying."

We were beating around the bush, and I desperately needed to get down to it before I lost my nerve. I cleared my throat, adjusting in my seat and pulling a throw pillow in front of me to hug. "Ryan, we need to talk, and I need you to be completely honest with me."

His face grew ashen. "Okay…" I took a gulp of my wine, draining the glass and setting it on the table. Liquid courage, they called it. We'd see. "About today?"

"Sort of," I said vaguely. "There's something I've been meaning to talk to you about for, well… a long time now. But, it's complicated."

"Just spit it out," he said, sitting up further. "You're freaking me out."

"You told me before that you quit drinking because you got reckless in your twenties," I said matter-of-factly. "But you never explained what that meant, exactly."

He seemed taken aback, the conversation coming out of nowhere for him.

"What does that have to do with anything?"

I folded my hands together. "Can you just tell me what happened?"

"I *have* told you. I was wild there for a while. It was a crazy time, and I was your typical twenty-something kid. I just… I can't explain it. I made horrible decisions, barely made it through college, spent most of my nights drunk off my ass with people I didn't know and most of my days with debilitating hangovers. One day I woke up and realized I needed to get my shit together. So, I did."

I pressed my lips together, studying him. "Just like that?"

His skin was paler than I'd expected. He was nervous. Understandably so, but it was odd to see him so rattled. "I mean, basically, yeah. Why?"

I sighed, feeling frustrated with him. *Why can't he just tell me the truth? Why is he going to make me say it?*

"I thought you swore there were no secrets between us," I said, twisting my lips in frustration. If he was able to lie about this, who knew what else he'd lied about.

"There aren't." He scoffed, setting his drink down and reaching for my hands. I kept them folded together on top of the pillow.

"I know the truth," I said finally, my voice barely above a whisper as chills ran over my arms. My words seemed to hang in the air between us, like a grenade that had the potential to detonate and tear us apart.

"What are you talking about?" He gave an uneasy smile, but it disappeared in an instant. "The truth about what?"

"I know why you quit drinking." Tears pricked my eyes. "I know what you did."

"What I did?" There was a new emotion on his face I didn't quite recognize. *Anger.* Or, what I assumed anger must look like on those features. I had seen it so rarely since I'd met him. Ever calm, ever patient, this dear husband of mine. "What do you mean?"

"I was there that night. *I saw you.*"

With that, he stood from the couch. He must've sensed the truth in my words, understood what I was telling him, but he didn't want to believe it.

"Saw me what?"

My lips pressed together, helping me to suppress the tears blurring my vision. "I should've told you sooner. I was angry and scared, and then… I loved you so much. I wasn't trying to. I wasn't planning to love you. But I did. I do. I've been so scared to have this conversation, but it's going to eventually come out, and I want you to hear it from me. I don't like secrets. You know that. And I want us to always be able to be honest with each other."

I stood too, walking toward him. He backed away slowly, shaking his head.

"What are you saying, Grace?"

"You know about Everleigh's sister, right?"

"The dead one?"

I winced at his harsh words. "Her name was Mariah Sinclaire," I told him. "They were stepsisters, different last names." I watched the emotion register on his face when I said her name. "You recognize the name, don't you?"

His jaw dropped, and there were tears in his eyes instantly. "What are you—" He didn't finish. There was no point. I'd said what I came to say. What I'd been trying to say for a year. He hung his head down. "How do you know?"

"Ryan, Mariah was my best friend. She'd been my best friend since college. We moved in together after graduation, even worked at the bookstore together for a while. We were walking home together that night; our apartment was just a few blocks from the bar, and the weather was nice enough that we thought it'd be okay. We'd both been drinking, but we weren't close to drunk. A car rounded the corner so fast, swerving all over the round, and she screamed and pushed me down—pushed me off the road and to safety—but she wasn't quick enough to save herself. They said she died instantly, but I swear I heard her crying afterward. I'll never forget the way she sounded."

I shivered as the terrible sounds came back to me, dusting a tear from the corner of my eye.

"The car kept driving, but I saw what it looked like. I saw your stupid 'Save the Whales' bumper sticker. I remembered it."

"I don't understand…" He was crying then, fat tears trailing down his cheeks.

"I told the police what the car looked like, but they never found you. Mariah died, and her killer was never brought to justice." I stared at him with growing disgust as the memory replayed in my mind. "Why didn't you stop? Why didn't you check on her?" I was crying harder then, tears streaming down my face as I stared at him, the weight I'd been carrying for so long finally easing.

"I-I—*damn it!*" He ran a palm over his face to dry his tears. "Why are you telling me this? Why are you doing this? What do you want? Are you going to turn me in? Leave me? Is that your plan? Do you hate me? Because, let me tell you, Grace, you can't hate me any more than I hate myself!"

I was still, letting the tears linger on my cheeks. "No. I don't hate you, and I'm not planning to turn you in," I said. "That's what I'm trying to tell you. I've been holding onto this secret for so long, letting it tear away at us, but I don't want to anymore. You've had to keep this part of yourself tucked away from me, but I don't want you to do that anymore."

I paused, trying to compose myself. I couldn't stop now. I had to tell him everything.

"A few months after it happened, I saw you. At the same stupid bar we'd left that night. When I saw your bumper sticker and noticed that your car had a brand-new bumper and headlight, I knew who you were and what you'd done. But I had no proof. I wanted to turn you in, but who would listen to me? The police had written me off as a drunk, irrational kid back then. If I was going to them again, I needed to know you better. I needed to be able to prove what I was saying. So, I started following you. Researching you. But as I learned more about you, I discovered you were, among other things, very rich."

"My parents are rich," he argued out of instinct, sniffling angrily. It was something I was learning all rich kids, but especially my husband, liked to say.

"Yes, and I discovered how well connected they were—your dad is a lawyer, for crying out loud. I had to be smart about my next moves. It sounds insane, but I'd followed you for years before I let you meet me. It wasn't by accident that you ran into me that day. I knew if I wanted to get you to admit what you'd done, I needed to get closer to you. But the thought was terrifying. I mean, you'd killed my best friend."

I stopped, trying to regain my resolve. "When you asked me out, I kept saying no because I wanted to keep focused. Because I hated you then, but I had to pretend not to in order to get justice for my friend. Eventually, though, I agreed because I intended to get close enough to you to find damning evidence. At the very least, I planned to make your life miserable." I sighed, pausing as I replayed those six months together. "But then, I fell in love with you, Ryan. It doesn't make sense. It shouldn't have happened, but it did."

He was trembling as he watched me tell the story, tears continuing to cascade down his cheeks. Did it haunt him like it had me? Did he have nightmares about that night? From what I'd seen, he seemed to sleep rather peacefully.

"And once I fell for you, nothing else mattered. I saw how hard you were working to create a better life for yourself. Watched you get sober. Watched you try to be a better person." I sniffed, dabbing at my eyes again. "I'm not sure I can ever forgive you for what you did, but I want you to know that I do love you. Despite it all. Despite your demons. Despite my own. It's why I appreciate you taking such good care of me. I'm not easy to be married to, but you make it look effortless. You never make me feel guilty for what you have to put up with. For all of my worry and fear."

"You shouldn't have to feel guilty about it," he said. "You're a good person, Grace. The best person." He stepped toward me then, reaching for my hand. I rested it on his palm as he wept. "You deserve someone better than me. I'm awful. Horrible. I'm a murderer, Grace. That woman... Mariah... she didn't deserve to die. I was so stupid... so selfish. How can you stand to look at me knowing what I've done?"

"Because I love you." The answer came out in a breath.

The crease in his forehead deepened. "But how can you?"

"Love doesn't always make sense," I said simply. "But you've been slipping lately. Drinking more and more. You seem stressed. I wasn't sure I was ever going to tell you. I don't want you to worry that I think less of you, but I want to be honest. I don't like secrets. I don't want you to have to lie. It's why, when I saw you not wanting to go to the police, I realized how much it must haunt you—what you did. The fear of being caught every single day. That's why you didn't want to go, isn't it? Because being around the police makes you nervous?" The wine was giving me courage I wouldn't have had otherwise, and I couldn't help being invigorated by it. Now that I'd let the secret out, it was like a dam had been opened. Suddenly I could say everything I was thinking and feeling.

He pressed his lips together, his eyes darting back and forth between my own as he appeared to contemplate what to say. "It wasn't that, really. But you're right; it was because of what I'd done."

He sucked in a deep breath. "I need you to listen to me, Grace. And believe me when I say that night was the darkest night of my life. I'd been drinking, yes. I'd had a fight with a friend, and I wasn't paying attention. It was dark, and I rounded the corner too fast... I didn't see your friend until it was too late. I heard the scream, felt the thump, and then it was over. Next thing I remember, I was pulling over several miles up the road. My heart was pounding, my whole body shaking. I remember vomiting up everything in my stomach. Then, I left. I was scared. The car was damaged. I was just waiting for the police to come and arrest me. I knew it would happen sooner or later."

He shook his head, wiping his eyes forcefully. "It should have happened. I should've gone to jail. But it didn't happen. They didn't come. No one asked any questions. I'd gotten off. Maybe I should've turned myself in. I thought about it, but I was scared. I didn't want to go to jail. I'm not a bad person. I didn't want one bad decision, one second of my life, to ruin the rest of it. I hadn't done it on purpose. I shouldn't have been drinking, and definitely shouldn't have been driving, but it was a mistake."

He was crying again, silently, shiny streamers of tears painting his pale cheeks. "I made a horrible mistake, and it didn't ruin my life. I was lucky. The thought of going to the police and potentially getting some dumb teenager into trouble for goofing off and making a mistake? It seemed hypocritical and wrong. We can fix the windshield. I didn't want to see anyone get arrested for something so simple, especially if it was an accident—which I still choose to believe it was."

I nodded. That thought hadn't crossed my mind, but it made sense. "I understand. I'm sorry you couldn't tell me that before."

His eyes widened. "Does Everleigh know?"

My throat grew tight. "No. And I'd never tell her. It wouldn't do anyone any good. I'm protecting you, Ryan, because I love you, but also because I love her. Tearing open her wounds when she's just starting to heal isn't something I'm interested in doing, even if you weren't the person in that car. I want Everleigh to move on with her life, and bringing it all back up would only set her back further. I wouldn't have agreed to marry you if I had any intention of telling her what you did or turning you in. She can *never* know. That's another reason why I felt like I had to go ahead and talk to you now. I've been careful never to mention Mariah's name around you, but between Everleigh and me, I knew it was just a matter of time before you heard her name and put it together. I was afraid *you'd* leave *me* out of fear."

He pulled me into a hug. "No. I'd never leave you, Grace. I'm just so sorry. I'm sorry for any pain I caused you, for taking your friend away. I've tried so hard to make up for it every day of my life. It's why I work so hard to protect you, because I couldn't protect her. It's part of what's made me the way I am. I realize now how quickly everything can end. How quickly the people we love can be taken away."

His shoulders shook with sudden, inconsolable sobs. "I'd do anything to go back to that night and fix what I did. *Anything.* All I can do is try to be better, and I do. I give back every chance I can. I donate, I volunteer. I try to be selfless. To live in honor of her. I want to be a better man than I was that night. For you. For her. I meant what I said earlier, Grace. I don't know what I'd do if I ever lost you."

"You're not going to lose me," I told him, squeezing my arms around his chest. When we broke apart, I cupped his face, swiping away his tears. "I'm here. I'll always be here. I love you."

He choked back a sob. "You'd really stay with me knowing all of this? Knowing what a monster I am? You love me that much?"

"I *have* stayed with you knowing all of this. I love you so much that nothing else matters. You aren't a monster. You made a mistake. I see how good your heart is, Ryan. I see you giving back—helping Everleigh whenever she needs it, taking care of me, even helping that man in the woods. I may not always understand your motivation, but I know it comes from someplace good. I know that you're good, okay? I'm just glad we could clear the air about what happened, for both of our peace of mind, but I would never tell a soul what you did. I *will* protect you at all costs."

He nodded, his chin quivering. "I'm sorry for what I did. I'm sorry about Mariah. There isn't a day that goes by that I don't think about her... what I cost her..."

"Shh... it's okay." A lump formed in my throat at the thought of her, and I swallowed it down. She was gone, and he was here. I didn't have to choose between them. The choice had already been made for me.

CHAPTER THIRTEEN

Ryan

We stayed up most of the night, talking about what had happened. I was crying a lot—too much. She was a saint. How could she forgive me for doing such unthinkable things? And, worse, what if she hadn't? What if she thought she had, but she would eventually change her mind? What if this was thrown back in my face during every argument? What if we had a nasty divorce someday and she chose to tell everyone then? She thought she'd relieved me of the secret, but all she'd done was prove that someone else out there knew it.

Since that night, I believed I controlled the secret. The darkest moment of my life. I foolishly believed it would die with me. But I'd been wrong. What was I supposed to do with that?

I'd meant what I said—I had tried to right the wrong that I did that night. I have tried. For years, I've worked to get sober, to clean up my act, to give back to those in need, to always protect those I cared about. I wanted nothing more than to be a good person, a good husband, a good employee. It didn't make what happened right, but it was the least I could do. Was it enough? For her? For me? I just didn't know.

As I lay in bed, my mind reeling with so many questions I didn't have answers to—may never have answers to—Grace lay next to me, sound asleep. Every once in a while, a soft snore could be heard from her side of the bed. Everything she did was precious.

Despite the danger she posed to me now, I couldn't help being enchanted by her.

My fascination was borderline obsessive, I knew. But who said being obsessed with your wife was a bad thing? You wouldn't hear me complaining about a second of it. She was my person, my best friend. The one I wanted to spend every waking moment with. When Grace and I had first started dating, my friends and family had complained that I stopped seeing them as much, and I couldn't defend myself because it was true. I had. But it was because I knew how right Grace and I could be together. Because I felt as if getting this relationship right would be a form of penance for the life I'd taken. Grace had a rough life before me, and I was determined to make sure the rest of her life was better. Because of me. She was my salvation. She was the only thing keeping me afloat.

No one else mattered to me like she did, and I had to prove that to her. Looking back, I hadn't talked to those friends in months, some well over a year. Grace had become my whole life—what would I do if it all fell apart? What would I have left?

A knock on the door jolted me completely awake. I sat up, my body pulsing with ice-cold fear. The clock on the nightstand showed it was just after eight that morning. Who could be at the door?

The man from the woods? Teenagers who had come to apologize for the car? The police? Every time someone knocked on the door or the phone rang with an unfamiliar number, I worried it would be someone with the news that what I'd done had been found out. I'd spent the past few years worrying that someone would find out who I was, what I'd done. Every person who stared at me a little too long in a crowd. Every time I turned on the TV and heard 'breaking news.' Every time a police car drove through our subdivision. It never goes away—the worry, the fear. How had I not realized I'd already been found out, and it was by the person I hoped to fool the most? Grace may know my secret, but she could never know how much I worried about getting caught. I wouldn't let her see it, even now. She was too important. She had to be protected from that side of me. Worry didn't exude strength. Panic didn't scream confidence.

As the knock came again, I moved quicker, standing up from the bed. I was still dressed from the night before, so I hurried across the room without having to throw on clothes. Grace stirred, rubbing her eyes gently. "What is it?" she whispered. "Where are you going?"

"Someone's at the door." I opened the bedroom door and stared at the glass of the front door where the knocking was coming from. A man's outline could be seen through the glass, blurry from the frosted, beveled surface. For a split second, my stomach lurched, and I feared the worst.

Then, I realized with a flood of relief who it was. The sheriff. From the day before. I searched my brain for his name. *Ritter.* That was it.

I hurried across the room and pulled open the door, staring at him with shock and confusion. Why was he back? Had something happened? Had he found something? His car had definitely been gone the day before, and he hadn't stopped in to tell us that anything was going on. Then I saw Andrea.

"Good morning!" she cried, chipper as ever. "Sorry, did we wake you? We tried to call, but service is God-awful up here." She held out the keys to our car with her long, red nails, and I glanced behind her to where it sat, a brand-new windshield already installed.

"It's done? Really? *Wow.* Thank you." I'd sort of been expecting there to be an issue getting it to us on time, but I didn't say as much. I heard Grace's careful footsteps behind me. She'd wrapped a robe around herself when she appeared next to me, her hair still messy from sleep.

"Yep, it's all done. Tony had time to get it fixed yesterday evening, and your insurance took care of the cost, so you guys are good to go."

"Thank you," I said again. I reached for my wallet on top of the microwave and pulled out a twenty-dollar bill. "Here, let me at least offer you something."

"No"—she waved it away—"you don't need to do that. You don't owe a thing. Like I said, it was totally covered. Your insurance should be sending you something to let you know what they paid."

"I know. But consider it a tip. You went above and beyond, and we really can't thank you enough." She looked as though she were going to argue again, but Grace spoke up first.

"Please. We insist. Ryan's right. If you hadn't made sure we had a ride home and then delivered our car to us, I'm not sure what we would've done. It's the least we can do."

Andrea took the bill, looking bashful. "Well, thank you. We certainly haven't been immune to this terrible economy, so we appreciate it." She folded it and slid it into her pocket.

Beside her, Sheriff Ritter cleared his throat, drawing our attention to him. "So, how did everything go last night? You never called, so I'm assuming there was no trouble?"

"Nope, no trouble at all," I said. "It was a quiet night. I guess you were right about it just being a one-off with some rowdy kids."

"Mhm. Well, good."

"Did you find anything in the woods that would help you figure out what may have happened, though? Was the man still living down by the stream? Did you get a chance to question him?" Grace asked.

"I did find what looked like remnants of a camp near the area that you described. A tent that had fallen over, some discarded trash and the like, but there was no one there. If the man was staying there at one time, I don't think he is anymore."

He cleared his throat as I let out a small sigh of relief, looking at Grace.

The sheriff went on, "I found a few beer cans on the route into the woods, leading me to believe there could've been kids out there recently, like we'd suspected, but my deputy drove around the woods and into the driveway a few times last night and said there were no signs of trouble. It seems like whoever it was is long gone now. I'm sorry it happened to you, but I'm glad it seems to be all taken care of. I don't anticipate that you'll be having any trouble for the rest of your stay."

I felt the tension leaving my neck and shoulders at the news that the man had left. Hopefully, it would bring my wife some peace as well. "Well, thank you for checking it out, Sheriff," I said. To my left, Grace nodded.

"Yes, we really appreciate you looking into it."

"Just doing my job. I'm glad it was nothing too serious, and I hope you folks enjoy the rest of your vacation." He tipped his head toward us, and Andrea grinned.

"This area sure is nice," she agreed. "Now that you have your answer, I'd say you should be able to have quite a bit of fun out here."

"We're actually planning to go ahead and head for home early," Grace said. "This morning. We appreciate all you've done for us. It just still doesn't feel safe enough for us to stay."

"I understand," Sheriff Ritter said. "But I certainly wish that wasn't the case."

"This is such a beautiful little cabin," Andrea added, a pout on her lips as she looked up toward the roof and back down, taking in the sight. "I wish it was better taken care of and that we could get people here because of something other than its history."

"It seems like the owner may be trying," Grace said. "When my husband rented it, there was no mention of what happened here in the ad."

They lowered their brows. "Yeah, that's right. You did mention that yesterday," Andrea said. "It still seems odd to me." We were met with a moment of silence before the sheriff patted the door's frame with a loud sigh.

"All right, well, we'd better get back into town. Safe travels back home." With that, he stepped back off the porch and, together, he and Andrea made their way back to his cruiser. I fumbled with our keys in my palm, watching and waving as they backed out of the driveway before I shut the door.

Once they were gone, I placed the keys onto the countertop, still amazed that things had gone so smoothly. When I glanced over my shoulder, Grace was staring at me. "I'm in shock a little bit. That was so quick. Was she sure the insurance covered everything? We didn't even owe a deductible?"

"Apparently so, yeah. She said they'll contact us, so we'll know for sure then, but that's the way it sounded. Good news, after all, hm?" I made my way further down the counter, where a box of cherry danishes sat and pulled one out, taking a bite. My throat was dry from the night before, the sour taste of wine on my breath. I turned to face Grace. "Do you still want to head home?"

She was nodding before the question had even left my mouth.

"Okay. Fair enough. We'll have breakfast, get a shower, and then hit the road."

"Thank you," she said, though there was no need to thank me. I'd picked a horrible vacation spot where she'd not been allowed to rest and relax for even one day. If anything, she should be furious with me. I wanted her to be able to have a bit of fun, but judging by the look on her face, I knew it was unlikely she'd agree to stay a moment longer.

I took another bite of the danish. "I've been thinking… We should make one last good memory here before we head out.

Something small. Now that we know he's gone and there's no one out there. What do you say? One last quick dunk in the hot tub first?"

She looked toward the window, one arm wrapped around herself. "I'd rather not. I just want to get out of here, honestly. Get home." Again, she looked down, and I wondered what she was thinking, though I suspected it had something to do with our newfound knowledge of what had happened here.

"Okay." I couldn't contain my disappointment, but I had no right to say so. She was right—we should leave. More than that, I had no leverage to say what was right or wrong anymore. She held all the power because of what she knew. I'd always done my best to avoid disagreements with her—I wanted nothing more than to keep her happy—but now I'd have to work even harder. With my secret as her leverage, I'd have to prove how grateful I was, how deserving, every single day.

Then a horrible thought struck me. What if she actually had told Everleigh about what I'd done? She'd said she hadn't, but could I be sure? She'd kept this secret so well, after all. And, even if she hadn't yet, what if she was eventually going to? She'd told me once that when she swore not to tell our secrets, that didn't include Everleigh. She knew about all our problems, our sex life, our struggles to get pregnant. There wasn't anything she didn't know, so why would I assume Grace had kept this to herself? I had no reason to believe it other than because I wanted to take her at her word.

If she'd told Everleigh, that would make three people who knew my secret, including myself. It was getting out of hand. And, on top of that, the fact that Everleigh was Mariah's sister was gut wrenching. *If she knows, she must hate me...*

She couldn't know, I realized.

She was too kind to me. She trusted me too much. Our friendship had grown because of how close she and Grace were. If she knew what I'd done, how could she stand to look at me? To be in the same room as me? It just didn't make sense.

I needed it to not make sense because I needed it to not be true.

As my mind raced, Grace turned to walk from the room. "I'll start packing." I nodded—at least I think I did. I was too busy thinking. Worrying. Stressing the fuck out.

What was I going to do? This changed everything. As much as I loved her, as much as I never wanted to lose her, the dynamic had changed. She had too much power now. She was dangerous. But would she use that? I just didn't know.

"Ryan!" Her frightened voice shook me to my core. I dropped the pastry onto the counter and rushed toward the bedroom.

"What's wrong?" I demanded.

She met me in the doorway, her face ashen. "Did you move our phones?"

I shook my head. "No. They should be on the nightstands. We plugged them in to charge last night."

"Yeah," she confirmed, her expression unchanging. "And now they're gone."

CHAPTER FOURTEEN

Grace

"Our phones are gone. They aren't on the nightstands. They're missing," I repeated, staring at his stunned face. He rushed past me, as if I might be mistaken, and made his way toward my bedside table. Then, he looked across the bed toward his.

"Where could they have gone?"

"I don't know," I said. "Were they there when you got out of bed earlier?"

"I didn't… I mean, I don't know. I wasn't paying any attention. I think so, though. I feel like I would've noticed if they were missing." His eyes were wide as he stared around in disbelief, pressing his fingers to his temples.

"Okay, well, maybe we just *thought* we plugged them in? We were both drinking quite a bit last night. Maybe we just planned to and then got distracted and didn't get the chance. They could've fallen down beside the bed, or maybe we laid them somewhere…" It didn't make sense, but then, nothing about this did. "They have to be around here somewhere." Ryan was already overturning pillows, ripping off sheets and pillowcases. He looked under the bed. I opened the drawers of the nightstand, moving around a travel guide and book of expired coupons. The dressers were completely empty, aside from a broken hanger and a ball of dried-up dryer sheets.

"Did we go downstairs?" I asked. "Or leave them in the living room, maybe?"

He shook his head, but darted in that direction anyway, while I made my way into the bathroom. I searched under the sink, in each of the drawers, even opened the shower, though I knew there'd be no reason for them to be there.

As I closed the shower door, I froze, hearing the sounds of the car alarm from the driveway.

Not again.

I grabbed hold of the doorframe, bracing myself for what was to come, and made my way out of the bedroom and toward the kitchen. Ryan was standing at the top of the stairs in the living room, his eyes wide. When he saw me, his panicked expression transformed to a grimace.

Neither of us asked the question I knew was on our minds, but instead turned our focus to the door, the blaring of the car alarm loud and obnoxious. He pushed his way in front of me, one arm outstretched to keep me back, though I was having none of it. I grabbed the keys from the table and pressed the button to end the noise.

He reached for the door handle, twisting the lock. I watched his shoulders rise and fall with a heavy breath, and then he swung the door open it in one swift motion.

We stepped out onto the porch in unison, both surprised and relieved to see that our windshield appeared fine. So, what had caused the commotion, then?

I looked to our left, then right, my heart thudding loudly in the silent woods.

With every step Ryan took toward the car, I followed, our pacing almost in unison as we made our way down the steps and onto the gravel. When we drew near the car, he stopped abruptly, as did I.

"Ryan..."

"What the hell…"

We stood, staring at our car—our only getaway—and the slashed tires it sat upon. We had no phones. And now we had no car.

"This wasn't kids. This was the man. It had to be. We're trapped," I whispered, seeing the terror on my husband's face and knowing he realized it, too. "Right where he wants us. And the police think we're leaving this morning."

Ryan cursed under his breath, and his face became instantly serious as our predicament became clear. He jumped into action, pushing me forward, back up the stairs and through the open door. "Get inside," he said, though we were already in. He locked the door behind us, panting heavily. "We need to find our phones."

I nodded. "Yes."

"We have to call the sheriff."

"Did you see them downstairs? I've searched all over the bedroom and bathroom."

He ran a shaking hand over his chin. "I'd just searched the living room. I hadn't made it down there before the car alarm started going off. I'll go look now. Will you be okay up here?"

I nodded, my stomach in knots. "I'll double check up here."

He looked back toward the door, putting a hand on the lock to check it once more before kissing my cheek and rushing past me. "I'll be right back." He hurried down the stairs and, after a moment, I made my way back into the bedroom, glancing out every exposed window as I went.

He was still out there. I just knew it.

Waiting.

Watching.

Once in the bedroom, I headed straight for my suitcase, but froze as I heard something behind me. "Ryan…?"

But even as I spoke, I knew it wasn't my husband.

The soft shuffling of feet, a haggard, raspy breath. Slowly, the closet door started to move. Everything seemed to slow down as I stood rooted to the spot.

I couldn't make my feet move. Instead, in the reflection of the mirror across the room I watched the door slide open.

Then the man from the woods appeared, his dirty face peeking through the crack. The right corner of his mouth upturned slightly in a wry grin, no doubt taking pleasure in catching me off guard and alone.

He held a knife in his hands—most likely the one he'd used to flatten our tires— outstretched toward me as he made his way out of the closet. I released a bloodcurdling scream as I finally spun around, backing away from him.

"No, please!"

He took a step toward me, his eyes narrowing. There was darkness in them. The same darkness I'd seen before. Though Ryan thought the man was harmless, I'd known differently. I'd known this would happen.

"How did you get in here?" I begged. "What do you want from us?" *Where is Ryan?*

I heard my husband's footsteps thunder as he ran back up the stairs. The man lunged at me without a word. I ducked out of the way, trying to stay on my feet. Up close he was old and frail. Not as quick on his feet as I was. But the knife held its own weight. If he managed to catch me, it would be over. My heart raced in my chest, my body tingling with the lightning of adrenaline that raced through my veins as I moved, once again, out of his reach.

He growled, and I caught a whiff of him as he moved nearer. He smelled dirty—of rot and decay. My stomach tensed, and I forced myself to breathe through my mouth. When he lunged for me the next time, my back slammed into the wall, stopping me from moving. His hands grabbed hold of the sleeve of my shirt, dirt-caked fingernails showing it had been long since they'd been trimmed. He stared at me, raising the knife chest-level.

"What do you want?" I asked again, louder this time, as I heard Ryan growing nearer. *Hurry.*

"Grace!" Ryan called, his voice nearing the bedroom. "What's going on?"

"Do you want money? We can give you mo—" The man raised the knife to my throat, and I stopped talking. This was it. The end. My life was ending. I was going to die right here. I closed my eyes, accepting my fate as I smelled his foul breath and felt the cool sting of the knife land on my skin.

I expected it to be sudden, but he seemed to be taking his time as he drew the knife's blade down my neck and toward my collarbone. What was he doing? Did he plan to make it quick? Or would he draw it out? Would I suffer? I'd be just another folk legend—a woman who'd died in the cabin like the two women before her. Would he kill Ryan, too? He was a witness—

"Hey!"

I heard the heavy, hurried footsteps that said my husband had made it into the room, and then the hands were jerked away from me, and I heard a grunt. I opened my eyes, shocked to see Ryan's hands around the man's neck. The man swiped and stabbed at the air, trying to wriggle free of his grasp, but his feeble body was no match for my husband. Ryan shoved him forward, and the man dropped the knife, searching around for it on the ground once he'd steadied himself. Ryan was quicker, kicking the knife back toward me. *"Get in the bathroom, Grace! Lock the door!"* he said, the vein in his temple throbbing.

I stared at the knife, but I didn't move. I was frozen, overcome with emotion: fear, anger, relief that my end hadn't come just yet.

As Ryan took a step toward him, the man scrambled to stand up, hurrying out the door, knife forgotten. I heard his footsteps as he fled out of the cabin, Ryan close behind him. Then I heard the door shut. *Am I alone? Did Ryan leave me alone in the cabin?*

I swallowed, staring down at the knife again with a heavy sense of dread. Panic gripped at my organs, wrapping them in its spidery fingers. This time, I bent down to pick it up with shaking hands. The handle was caked with dirt, as his clothes and hands had been. I didn't bother dusting it off, instead turning it over and holding it out as if it were going to be enough to protect me. As if I knew a thing about using it.

The sound of footsteps rushing back toward me caused me to freeze, lifting the knife in the air, stretching it out and praying I'd be fast enough, strong enough. My breathing quickened as they grew nearer. *No. Please no.*

Before I had time to worry too much, Ryan was back in the doorway, his face red, chest heaving. He reached for the knife in one quick motion, took it from my hands, and slipped it into his back pocket. His arms went around my shoulders, letting me fall into his chest. My sobs came then, loud, frightened, and inconsolable. The reality of what had happened hit me square in the chest. *I almost died.* He'd almost killed me. He'd almost killed Ryan.

Ryan was trembling against my body, and I knew how scared he must've been. *How did this happen? How did he get inside?* Nothing felt safe anymore. I felt exposed. How long had he been hiding in our bedroom?

"He's gone," he whispered. "You're safe. He's gone."

"You saved my life," I whispered through my tears. "Ryan, you saved me. He was going to kill me."

"I wanted to kill him, Grace. When I saw him in here, when I saw him with you, I wanted to kill him. I think I would've if I'd caught up with him." He whispered it into my ear, his hot breath on my skin a warning. What he'd done before, he was capable of doing again, it said. But I couldn't think too closely about that. "My God, I was so scared."

"I was, too. I didn't know where you were. I don't know where he came from or how he got inside." I sobbed, burying my face further into his T-shirt.

"I'm so sorry. God, I feel like this is all my fault. I should've never offered him anything. I should've listened to you. I should've gotten you away from here—away from that man, away from this place. You asked me to, and I just acted like you were overreacting. I should've trusted your instincts. I almost got you killed. I would've never forgiven myself. God. I'm so sorry, Grace. *Fuck.* I'm so sorry."

I pulled back, brushing his hair out of his face and shaking my head, my hands were still trembling terribly, though my voice was steadier. "It's okay… It's all going to be okay. You didn't mean for this to happen. You… you saved my life, Ryan. That's all that matters. No one could've known what he was capable of. This isn't your fault."

He pushed his lips to mine, trying to reconnect us, to reassure himself that we were both okay. He breathed me in like a lifeforce, then rested our foreheads together. "I don't ever want to be that scared of losing you again. I can't—I can't lose you."

"You won't," I vowed. "We just need to figure a way out of here."

"Right. Yeah." He ran a hand over his face, inhaling sharply through his nose. "We need a plan. We have to find a way out of here."

"How do you think he got in?" I asked, shivering as I watched Ryan processing what had happened. He began pacing the room, looking around.

"I have no idea. He must've come in when we were outside… The door was standing open."

"It was all a setup," I said, realizing it then. The thought was chilling. I pictured him watching us make our way toward the car, him sneaking along the side of the cabin and inside just behind our backs. "But why? What does he want? I offered him money… We don't have much of anything to give him."

"I have no idea," he admitted. "I wish I did." He looked toward the nightstands. "Do you think he could've taken our phones?"

A chill crawled down my spine, and I brushed a hand over my arms, swiping away the goosebumps. "But how could he have? They were missing before. He would've had to come inside, take the phones, go back out to slice the tires and set off the alarm, then come back in to hide in the closet. If that's possible, it means he must have a way inside we don't know about."

Ryan's eyes lit up. "Wait, he was hiding in the closet?"

"Yes. He came through that door." I gestured toward the closet door where I'd seen him emerge, and Ryan approached it slowly. He pulled the door open at a snail's speed—it felt like he was moving it an inch per minute. When it was completely open, he moved over a few disheveled blankets that were knocked from their pile on the floor, sliding the hangers from one end to the other. He pressed on the wall in the back gently, then applied more force.

"There's nothing here. No signs that he's been here other than the smell…"

"Well, that's where he was. He charged right at me. I didn't have time to think or react or call for you…"

"I know, honey, I believe you. I was just hoping there'd be some clue as to who he is or how he got inside, if not through the front door."

"Or why he broke in here in the first place," I added. "What do you think he'll do with our phones? I have my passwords saved on there, our online banking, everything!"

He inhaled, his expression blank as he walked back over to the bed and zipped his suitcase. He pulled the phone charger from the wall and tucked it into the side of the suitcase. "I don't know, Grace. We'll figure that out eventually. But we both have passcodes, so he shouldn't be able to do anything with them. He doesn't exactly seem like the type who would know how to hack a phone or have the technology to do so. He's probably just going to try to sell them to get some extra money. When we get home, we'll clear our phones using the computer and order us both new ones. My biggest concern is just getting us away from here. Getting you someplace safe."

"How are we going to do that? Without cars or phones?"

His face grew ashen as he met my eye. "I don't know, Grace. I really don't know."

"We're trapped," I said again, a question in my words because I desperately didn't want to believe it. But the answer was there in his expression.

We are trapped.

There was no way out.

CHAPTER FIFTEEN

Ryan

We were trapped.

The tires now had deep gash marks running across their tread.

He had stolen our phones.

We were alone.

In an unfamiliar place.

We were going to die.

I couldn't bear to look at my wife, who was counting on me to say something. To do something. I needed to formulate a plan, even if it sucked.

Grace clutched a hand to her chest, her face growing paler as she processed what had happened. "What are we going to do?"

I stared at her, then at the door. There was no answer. No solution that made for a clear path, or even reasonable way forward. The truth was, no matter which way we went, we were in trouble. "If we stay in here, he could get bored eventually and leave."

"Or he could force his way in."

I nodded. "But if we go back out, he'll definitely catch us." I moved away from the door, pulling her with me as I lowered my voice. "It's two against one, so I like our odds better than his, and I still have his knife, but we just don't know what he's capable of. We have no way to call for help with our phones missing, even if we had service…" I shook my head, looking around the room to try and make a quick decision. Though I knew he couldn't see us where we stood, I somehow felt like I was being watched. And then there was the small matter of how he ended up in the cabin in the first place. I wanted to believe he'd come in when we'd been distracted looking at the tires, but if he'd been inside the cabin earlier this morning, early enough to take our phones, there was a good chance he still had a way in.

Without further thought, I headed for the stairs toward the lower level, unable to move my body fast enough. "Make sure all the doors and windows are locked!" I shouted. We should've done it earlier. My heart thudded as I darted down the stairs. I could hear Grace moving about upstairs, and I focused on the sound. As long as she was moving, she was safe. As long as I didn't hear her scream, she was okay.

I triple checked the glass door that led to the first-floor patio then slowly made my way to the bathroom. I put my hand on the wood of the door, counting to three in my head before forcing it open. I'd almost expected him to be there, but to my great relief, it was empty and dark. No beady eyes or scraggly hair in sight.

I gasped as the cool breeze hit me from behind the blind. Had I never realized the window down here was open? Or had this been how he got in? I spun around. Up above me, I heard Grace continuing to bustle about. Hoping we'd just managed to overlook it, I slammed the window shut, turning the lock and securing it into place. Then I closed the blinds and retreated from the bathroom.

There were no blinds or curtains on the floor-to-ceiling windows on the entire wall surrounding the back door, the side looking out into the woods. Though it was daytime, and I should've been able to see him if he was out there, I flicked off the lights. I'd never felt so exposed. The beautiful windows where we had loved looking out at the trees now felt haunted. It was much like the strange, unfathomable feeling of standing naked in a crowd.

I grabbed the pool sticks from their mount on the wall, figuring we could use them for protection, if nothing else. Before I headed back up the stairs toward the top floor, I noticed the light that was coming from under a door beside them. I twisted the handle, though it remained locked. When we arrived, we thought it was strange that the door was locked and the light remained on, but we had decided it must've been where the cleaners kept their supplies, as it was the only room in the house with a locked door. But now, I wasn't so sure. Why *was* the door locked? What was beyond it? Why was the light kept on?

I made my way back up the stairs and into the living room. "Grace?" Had I heard her walking recently? I'd stopped paying attention. "Grace?" I repeated, seconds later when she hadn't responded.

When she reappeared from the bedroom, making me jolt, she stared at me a little strangely. "Everything's locked up; all the blinds are closed. What are you planning to do with the pool sticks?" Like the bottom floor, the entire wall to our right was made of glass, exposing us to the woods below. But I took some solace in being up there, knowing he'd have some trouble reaching us on the top floor, while the bottom floor and its walkout to the woods felt more open for attack.

"I thought we could use them as weapons," I said, holding one out to her. "They're heavy. We could hit him with it, at least."

She ran her finger along the chalked end, not looking sure. "Do you think he's still out there?" she whispered, a question I'd been doing my best not to think about.

I looked toward the balcony, where, if we stepped outside, we could look down over the woods, the hairs on the back of my neck standing up with fear. *Did he come back?* Was he just outside again? I swallowed, taking a step toward the door.

I had to protect her at all costs. I had to know what we were up against. As I reached for the door, pressing my hands to the glass, I looked down, half expecting him to jump into view as if we were in a horror movie. Instead, I stared at the empty porch down at the edge of the woods, my body trembling with relief as I spun back around to face her. "He's gone."

Her eyes widened. "Gone where?"

"I don't know, but he's not here."

"He'll be back," she said. "He's obviously not going to leave us alone until he gets what he wants… Whatever he wants." She stared at the stick in her hands. "Maybe we should make a run for it? Like you said, it's two against one. He's old. Weak. We have weapons. We're in good shape."

The idea of leaving the house *ever*, let alone right then, wasn't appealing. "I don't know. I think we should wait until we have more of a plan. The sheriff won't be coming back to check on us because we just told him we're heading out this morning. We're out here alone until… when? I mean, eventually, the cleaners will have to come, right? Or the next guests… someone. We have enough food to last until someone comes for us. I mean, even if we get outside, where are we going to go? It's at least a few miles to the main road from here, and even further to town. We have no idea where he is, and we could end up running straight toward him."

"That's always going to be the case, though, isn't it? We'll never know where he is. We can't just stay in here for the rest of the week not knowing when he'll appear next. For all we know, that's exactly what he's counting on. He could break back in any moment. At least if we try to leave, we could catch him off guard."

"What if we can wait for him to appear somewhere down in the woods? If we watch for him near the edge, then we can make a break for the opposite side." I swallowed. "We'll have to leave everything here—all our bags. We can't have anything weighing us down."

She didn't respond for a moment, staring out the window with a strained expression. "I just don't understand… What do you think he wants? Do you think he's *the* serial killer from before? The one that killed those other women?"

"I don't know," I said. "Maybe he just wants money. Or to scare us."

"Well, it's certainly worked," she said dryly. "Did you notice his…" She ran her fingers along her neck, without finishing the sentence. She didn't need to. I knew exactly what she was talking about. I could still see the poorly healed scars on the front of his neck. Stretched and tough layers of red and too-white skin across the front of his throat. As if he'd been attacked by a wild animal and had no medical care. I'd noticed them when we ran across him in the woods before. Then I'd felt sorry for him.

We all had scars, some just lurked beneath the surface.

Now, though, it made me wonder what had happened to give him the scars? Had it been another of his victims who had fought back, rather than an animal?

I nodded, unable to meet her eye. "Yeah."

"What do you think happened?"

"I have no idea." It was the least of my concerns, honestly. I just wanted to get her out of here. To safety.

"Maybe that's why he doesn't talk…" She was staring back out the window again. As if lost to her own thoughts. "We have to find a way to call for help. What if we can make it to the car, lock the doors, and blare the horn?"

"Then what?" I furrowed my brow. "Even if we can keep him out of the car, who's to say anyone would hear it? We're so far away from everything!" I cursed under my breath, rubbing my temple as a sudden headache began to come on.

"Well, we have to do *something!* We can't just sit here and wait for him to come back."

"I know, okay?" I snapped. "I'm trying to think." I hadn't meant to yell, but tensions were running high. I was frustrated, angry, terrified. I could never admit that to her. I had to keep strong. She had to know I was in control. I just wished I felt in control.

Just then, we snapped to attention as a nearly unrecognizable noise broke through the silence.

"Is that—" Her eyes widened, mouth slack-jawed.

"A phone," I confirmed, but it wasn't one of ours. And it was coming from downstairs.

CHAPTER SIXTEEN

Grace

The sound of the phone ringing sent fear tearing through my insides. I was ice cold, my heart racing as we made our way across the living room and toward the first floor.

"Hello?" Ryan called as we eased our way down the stairs. *Is the man down here? Is he waiting?*

Downstairs looked much the same to me. A small TV mounted in the corner. Two small couches and a rocking recliner. A pool table in the center of the room. A wall of glass and a door that led outside. The small bathroom to our left. The ringing had stopped then, and Ryan made his way toward the bathroom the way you'd approach a feral animal. His hand was outstretched, his steps wide. He used his fingers to push it open, pool stick at the ready. The room was dark. When he flipped on the light, I gasped, despite the fact that no one was inside.

He turned back to look at me just as the ringing came again. Its sound was loud, obnoxious, and terrifying in the silence that inhabited the house. I glanced behind me, back toward the stairs, in the direction of the ringing.

My heart sank as I realized immediately where the noise was coming from.

"The locked room," Ryan said, making the connection as soon as I did. He hurried past me, grabbing hold of the knob and twisting as if he expected it to suddenly be unlocked.

It was not.

Instead, he pulled on the knob, twisting and jerking it, the door trembling and quaking against his strength, but not giving in. He growled, pulling harder, his face growing red as he twisted with all his strength. *"Come on!"* he said, cursing aloud and kicking the door.

"Ryan…" I tried to reach for him. To calm him. He shrugged me off.

"There has to be a way." The ringing stopped again, giving us a moment's peace, though Ryan didn't give up. "If there's a phone in here, it's our way to safety. We have to find a way to get to it." He stepped back, sizing up the door. "I think I can kick it down."

"Be careful," I whimpered. The last thing we needed was for him to get hurt. He nodded, looking ready to charge, when a thought came to me. "Wait! Maybe we should try picking the lock first? Or looking for a screwdriver? What if we can take the handle off? I think I saw some tools in a drawer upstairs."

He exhaled heavily, rubbing his hands together. "Okay. Yeah, let's try that," he said. Together, we hurried back upstairs, sifting through drawers as I tried to remember where I'd seen the tools.

"Found them," Ryan cried, pulling open the drawer wider. Inside were long, metal skewers for roasting marshmallows, a large ladle, an extension cord, a hammer, two flathead screwdrivers, and a small Phillips head screwdriver. He pulled both types of screwdrivers out, examining their tips before deciding on which would work. Then, he shut the door and we hurried downstairs, but not before I'd grabbed the hammer too—just in case.

Back on the bottom floor, Ryan set to work, the end of the Phillips screwdriver shoved onto the head of the screw. As he turned it furiously, the phone began ringing again. Who was calling? And why? Why hadn't the phone rung up until that point? I dreaded the answer as much as I wanted to learn it.

Within minutes, he had the face of the knob off. He gave a little push to the opposite side, and I heard it clang on the ground on the other side. I stared at the now-open hole where the knob had been, watching as Ryan placed his fingers inside and, almost in slow motion, pulled the door open.

The room was a small, unexciting closet—disappointing for all the work we'd put into getting inside—filled with cleaning supplies, extra toilet paper, blankets, and tools. In the far corner, there was a vacuum, broom, and spray mop, along with a bucket. Attached to the wall, there was a white board with scrawled notes about cleaning.

Tubs: 1st, 3rd
Windows: 2nd, 4th
Pool table: 1st
Remotes: every week
Dishwasher: 1st, 3rd
Washer/Dryer: 2nd
Grill: Jan, Mar, May, July, Sept, Nov

The schedule was normal. Believable. As if only ordinary things happened here. A brown corduroy jacket hung on the side of one of the metal shelves, a pair of dusty, knee-high rubber boots just underneath them.

On the far shelf, my eyes landed on the subject of the noise. A white, cordless phone sat on its base, a blinking green light flashing whenever it rang. There was no caller ID, nothing to let us know who might be calling.

Ryan reached for the phone, hitting the button to answer the call and placing it to his ear. He stared at me, his face pale and fearful. "H-hello?" He waited, and I watched his expression, hoping to see relief.

Instead, it grew angry. "Who is this?" He paused. *"Hello?"* He cursed, pulling it away from his ear and pressing the button to end the call with a forceful thumb.

"Who was it?" I asked. "What did they say?"

"Nothing. It was just silence."

As I took it from him, he turned away, looking at the shelves. "I wonder what else is in here that we could use for protection…"

"We need to call the police." This time, he didn't argue, preoccupied with moving bottles of bleach and cleaner in order to find something that might help us.

"Yeah, yeah, go ahead," he said. It wouldn't have mattered to me either way.

I pressed the button to start dialing, lifting it to my ear to listen for the dial tone, to instead be met by the sounds of heavy breathing.

"Hello?" I demanded, cold chills lining my skin again. More breathing. Steady. Deep. Sinister.

He'd either called at the exact time I'd answered, or the call had never been disconnected somehow.

It was him. Somehow, I just knew it. He was enjoying it. Toying with us. Loving watching us fear him.

"What do you want from us?" I screamed. "What do you want?" I ended the call, tossing the phone back onto the shelf as I burst into tears. "He's never going to let us go, Ryan. He's never going to—"

Ryan pulled me into his arms, seeming calm and confident for the first time in a while, though it didn't appear that he'd found anything of interest on the shelves. "It's going to be okay."

"He was still there," I told him. "He's just going to keep calling. We can't call for help if he doesn't stop calling."

"He has to be calling from our cell phones, right? And he didn't take the chargers. Eventually, they'll die."

"When? *Tonight?* We can't stay that long, Ryan. I'll go crazy waiting that long. And he has both of our phones, so even if they each only have a day's charge, that could give him two days! And for all we know, he does have a charger. For all we know, he's not homeless at all. He could be calling from his house. I mean, how does he even have this number? How does he even know this phone exists? How could he be calling from our phones when he doesn't have the passcodes? Nothing about this makes any sense!"

"Calm down," he demanded, his hand rubbing forceful circles on my back as he willed me to breathe. "Grace, I know you're scared. I'm scared, too, but you have to calm down, okay? You getting this worked up isn't solving anything. We need to keep our common sense right now." He reached for the phone again.

"I'm going to keep trying to call out. Eventually, we're going to get through. We have to." He hit the button and pressed it to his ear. Then he lowered it and hit the button again. *"No.* No, no, no, no, no." He hit the button over and over again, pressing it to his ear and pulling it away, staring down at the phone in horror.

"What is it?" I asked, but I knew. I knew before he said the words.

His face was ashen, his eyes haunted as he met mine. He shook his head.

"The phone lines are out. He must've cut the wire."

I fell to the floor, wrapping my arms around my knees as I stifled a sob. "What are we going to do, Ryan?"

He stood still, seemingly frozen in place with dismay and confusion. No answer came, because there was no answer to give.

We were trapped. Waiting for death. Waiting for the game to end.

Eventually, he sank down beside me, resting a hand on my knee as a silent tear fell down his cheek. "We'll figure something out," he promised, not meeting my eye. It was powerless, void of meaning or belief. We both knew we wouldn't. Both knew this story was only going to end in tragedy.

As we sat in silence, now heavier and louder without the phone's incessant ringing, only one thing was clear about our future.

There was nothing left to figure out.

We were going to die.

CHAPTER SEVENTEEN

Ryan

When we finally left the room, the house was dark all around us. Night had fallen, despite the fact that it felt like the world had stopped somehow. My face was raw from crying, my chest tight with panic and anger. I had done this. I'd brought her here. Brought us into this mess. But I couldn't get us out of it.

Outside the windows, the night was pitch black, aside from a sliver of the moon, which could hardly be seen from the bottom floor. I flipped off the closet light quickly. He could've been standing just beyond the window, and we wouldn't be able to see him, though with the light on, he could see us clearly. I stood frozen, wondering where we were safer, if anywhere. Dark or light? Upstairs or down? Inside or out? There seemed to be no right answers.

Grace slid her hand into my palm, unable to hide the quiver of fear. I knew one thing for certain, and that was that I'd die fighting for her. If it came down to either of us, I would die a thousand times over to make sure she was protected. If I could take him out, even if it cost me everything, I would do it. For her. To save her life. To give her a life.

She was all that mattered to me. Somehow, in that moment, I found sudden, razor-sharp focus. I squeezed her hand, extending my finger in the direction of the light switch for the room. I flipped it on.

"What are you doing?" she asked breathlessly.

"We aren't going to do this," I told her. "I'm not going to let us stay here and be afraid anymore. If he wants us, he's going to have to come and get us, but I'm not going to let it happen easily." I was speaking too loudly, as if I thought he could hear us. Maybe, deep down, I did. I had no idea what this man was capable of, who he was, or what he wanted.

"I'm scared..." she whispered. I tugged at her hand, leading her up the stairs.

"You don't have to be afraid. I'm going to keep you safe no matter what. Come on... Come with me."

"Where are you taking me?" She took a cautious step toward the stairs, following me with apprehension. I smiled at her. Even with her wide eyes filled with absolute terror, she was so beautiful.

"I think we'll be safer upstairs. We can keep an eye out for him from there." The knife was still in my back pocket. I held onto the pool stick with one hand, her hand with the other. She'd laid her pool stick down in exchange for a hammer.

It didn't matter.

If I had any say in the matter, she wouldn't need to use it.

We climbed the stairs slowly, wondering what was waiting for us at the top. There was silence all around us, the only noise the sound of the creaking wooden stairs under our weight. The top floor was lit up, giving him a perfect view of us if that's what he wanted.

I reached out, flipping on the porch lights. We were done hiding. We were here, but we were going to do this on our terms. As we reached the top floor and I spun around to face her, I was more certain of my decision than ever.

I held out my hands for her, and she took a clumsy step backward, nearly falling. I caught her. "Careful."

She smiled at me uneasily. "I love you."

"I love you, too..." I whispered. It was because I loved her that this was what I had to do. The decision wasn't easy. It terrified me, frankly, but it was my job to make the hard decisions. My job to love her enough to take the risks. I laid the pool stick down and reached for the knife in my back pocket.

He was out there somewhere. Watching. Waiting.

And when he came, we'd be ready.

CHAPTER EIGHTEEN

Grace

We sat and we waited. For what, I had no idea. Ryan paced for a while. Then sat next to me. We stared out into the woods, though the dim porch light did little to give us a clear view of what we were seeing. I knew he was out there; knew he was watching us. How long would we have to wait? Until morning? Until the next evening? I hoped it would all end soon, but I didn't expect it.

Though it filled me with fear to know we were being watched, that he was calculating his next move, there was also a rage inside me I hadn't felt in a long time—maybe ever. My anxiety had shifted to a dark place of outright anger. How dare he do this to us? How dare he turn our honeymoon into this?

I thought of Stanley, my heart breaking at the thought of what would happen to him if we weren't around to take care of him. Then I thought of Everleigh, who might be the one to call and report that we'd never come home. Would she continue to order his medicine? Would she give him only organic treats? Would she be okay herself, after losing not only her sister, but then her best friend?

She'd sent Ryan the address; would she come out to look for us when we didn't come home, or would she call the police and let them find us instead? How many times would she try to call me before she gave up? Maybe the housekeeper would be the one to find us before any of that happened. I could only hope.

I wished there was a way to leave her a note, a thank you for sticking with me through so much. For taking care of me. Loving me. I wanted to say goodbye in my own way.

At that, it was my turn to pace. I stood up, trying to think as I walked the floors nervously. I felt Ryan's eyes on me, knew he was watching me move. He was nervous for me, as always. Wondering when I was going to crack, to break. Wondering when I'd need him to put me together again.

I walked into the kitchen, where our bags rested on the floor from earlier. I lifted mine to the table and unzipped it.

"What are you doing?" he asked, spinning around on the couch.

"Looking for a pen. I want to write a letter to Everleigh. Just in case we don't…" I trailed off, unable to finish that sentence. Ryan stood as I searched through the bags, freezing when my hand made contact with something solid and cool in my bag. Two *somethings*.

I gripped them, pulling them out of the bag and staring at my hands in shock. "Our phones?"

"What the hell?" Ryan asked at the same time.

"How did they get in my bag?"

"Where did they come from?"

"Did you check the bags before?" he asked.

"Of course," I said, staring down at the 'No Service' notification on their screens. "They weren't in here before. I'm sure of it."

"Well, that's not possible… They had to be. He hasn't been back inside the cabin. He hasn't been around our bags. And, even if he had, why would he return our phones to us?"

I handed Ryan's phone back to him as he hammered the questions out. I wasn't paying any attention. I couldn't register any more shock today.

All I could think was that at least now I had a way to write my final goodbye.

My mind seemed to come back to the present at the sound of Ryan's voice. "There aren't any recent calls from this phone. Are there any on yours? Where he could've called the house?"

I checked my call log, shaking my head. "No. But that's not surprising. He could've deleted them, I guess. I just don't see how he could've used our phones in the first place. We have no signal out here. We had to get miles up the road before the phones would work to call the insurance company and the garage and, even then, service was spotty."

Ryan's eyes lit up, and he glanced out the window. "There must be somewhere near here with service, then."

"What?" I froze.

"Somewhere out in the woods. There must be a place where we can get enough service to make a nine-one-one call. Maybe up further on the mountain." His jaw was set, and I knew the determined look on his face.

"You can't be serious."

"Someone has to go." His eyes deadlocked with mine.

"No, Ryan, it isn't safe."

"We don't have a choice." He stepped back, moving to look out the window without hesitation. "I'll leave you here with the weapons. The hammer, the pool sticks. I'll take the knife and go out into the woods to see if I can get a better signal. You can lock the doors behind me."

"But, if you're right in thinking that he found somewhere with service, used our phones to make the calls, and then brought them back to us, that means he's been inside the house again. That means he can get to us. If you leave me, he can get to me. Either he has keys, or there's another way inside. You can't leave me here, and it's not safe for you to be out there alone, either."

He took a deep breath, closing his eyes. "You're right. We have to go together."

"Are you crazy? We can't go out there in the dark in the middle of the night! That's just asking to be killed!"

His face crinkled with dismay. "You said it yourself… We're no safer in here, Grace. He could be in this house right now for all we know. We have to get out of here, and getting somewhere where we can call the police is our only option."

"But what if he catches us?" I cried.

"Then, we fight. And maybe we die. But those are no worse odds than we have in here," he reminded me. "We have to go, and we have to go now. This is our only option."

I took a deep breath. "Let me finish this text to Everleigh. It may be the last chance I have." Tears filled my eyes as I typed the last words I may ever get to say to my best friend. For all I knew, she may never get to see them, but I hoped somehow, if my cell phone ever made it to a place with service, the text would go through. A message from beyond the grave.

I want you to know how thankful I am for you. You're the best friend I've ever had, and I can't thank you enough for always taking care of me. I've tried to take care of you as well. I'm not sure if I'll ever see you again, but I didn't want our last goodbye to be our last. I want you to know that I'd do anything for you, Ev. You deserve nothing less. Please never forget that. I love you, friend. Take care of yourself and Stanley for me. XO.

I wanted to say more. There was so much I needed to say to her: words of comfort, advice, and wishes for her future. She was like the little sister I never had, and it broke my heart to think of her only having this as my goodbye, but it was all I had time for. It would have to do.

With that, I hit send, locking my screen as it struggled to go through. "Okay," I said, as Ryan stared at me impatiently. "Let's do this."

CHAPTER NINETEEN

Ryan

I grabbed my wife, knowing it may be for the last time, and pressed my lips to hers. I wanted to go out remembering that feeling. Remembering the taste of her. The scent. If I was going to die, I'd rather it be here and now in the kitchen of a strange cabin with her lips on mine than in the woods alone. In the woods, scared.

I thought, briefly, about a suicide pact. About ending our lives under our terms, rather than his, but forced the idea away. It didn't have to be like this. We weren't going to give up. We were fighters. We were going to fight until our last breath. I wouldn't let him hurt her.

When we broke apart, I rested my forehead on hers. "I love you," I whispered, closing my eyes to savor the moment. She needed to know how much I meant it. "With every fiber of my being, Grace, I love you."

"I love you, too." She choked out the words through her tears.

"We're going to run. As fast as we can. And when either of us gets service, we call the police. If we see him, *if he gets me*, I need you to promise me you won't stop running. Promise me you won't turn back for me—"

"Don't talk like that—"

"Promise me, Grace!" I squeezed her shoulders.

"I promise," she squeaked, wiping her tears with the back of her hand.

"All I care about is that you get out alive. You leave me if you have to. Just don't stop moving. No matter what." Again, she nodded, sniffling and shaking through her sobs. She picked up the hammer from the kitchen table. At least, if I died, she would always have this moment to hang onto. My final moment of bravery, where I offered my life for hers. "Ready?" I asked.

"As I'll ever be…" She sucked in a deep breath as I turned to face the door, twisted the lock, and heard it click. I put my hand on the doorknob.

BANG.

We froze. I glanced over my shoulder. "What was that?"

BANG. She flinched at the sound. I locked the door once again.

"Ryan!"

I shoved past her, making my way toward the stairs, toward the sound.

"It's coming from downstairs," I said, more to myself than anything. She obviously already knew that, as we both stared in that direction.

"He's down there."

"Stay up here," I warned. "Go to the bedroom and lock the door. Don't come out no matter what you hear."

She stayed still, frozen in fear. "No! Don't go down there. Now's the time to run!" she called. "Please, Ryan."

I wasn't listening. She was right, I knew, but it didn't stop me from descending the stairs. I needed to know what he was doing. What the noise was. As I neared the bottom of the stairs, I had my answer.

Like a rabid dog, he threw himself into the thick wall of glass. Over and over again, he launched his body against it. When he saw me, he stopped. His fists pounded on the glass, eyes wild and bloodshot, throat bulging red.

"What do you want?" I bellowed, rage overcoming me. *"What do you want from us?"*

I heard Grace's footsteps coming down the stairs behind me, but I could focus on nothing other than the man who'd come out of the woods and into our lives, seemingly set on ruining them.

Again, he pounded on the glass, his screams animal-like, more growls than anything. I watched the scars on his neck throb, the red and white of his skin pulsing, real as a heartbeat. When Grace came into view, I watched the man's eyes flick to her. As if something in him snapped, he grew wilder. Angrier.

He flung himself at the window again, his mouth open wide, rotten teeth on full display. Grace was crying, loud sobs causing her whole body to shake next to me, our arms brushing each time she moved.

He pointed at her, shoving his thin, dirty finger onto the glass as if we were in an aquarium tank. Or an exciting exhibit. I kept a hand in front of her, trying to protect her as I struggled to understand what was happening.

She stepped forward. Past me and toward the glass, the man's cries growing louder.

"Grace, wait—"

"What do you want?" she begged, her voice a soft whisper through her sobs. "Why can't you leave us alone?"

The man flung himself at the glass again. He couldn't hear her. There was no way. I could hardly hear her myself. "Grace, get back." I hurried forward, trying to stop her.

"*Janie…*" the hoarse voice came through the glass, its sound like nails on a chalkboard. "*In… in. Let… me… in.*"

"*What do you want?*" she demanded again; this time loud enough I was sure he'd heard. She spoke to him as if I weren't even there.

"*Let… me… in,*" the man cried again, his voice a hoarse whistle, the words barely audible. "*Let… me… in.*"

To my surprise, Grace reached for the doorknob in a trance-like state. I watched in horror, paralyzed by fear.

"No, wait! What are you doing?" As she turned the lock with a flick of her wrist, I lunged forward, locking it back.

She didn't answer, calmly reaching for the lock again with a defiant look on her face.

"Grace, stop—" I tried to turn the lock once more, but it was too late, she twisted the handle, swinging the door open with one swift motion. The man lunged forward, his hands in the air as he tossed himself at her. She lifted the hammer, bringing it down and slamming it into his face. He staggered backward; his expression confused as blood began trailing down his temple. She swung again. Once, twice, three times.

She fell to the ground on top of him, despite the fact that he was putting up no fight.

Again.

Again.

She brought the hammer down onto his face, blood splattering onto her body and across the room. I watched in horror before snapping to reality and lunging forward, grabbing hold of her arm. *"Grace! Stop!"*

She stopped then, wide-eyed and nearly delirious as she stared up at me.

I looked down at him, his face a bloodied mess. My wife was covered in his blood, little flecks in her hair, her eyelashes.

"He's dead," I said, nodding slowly as I tried to pull the hammer from her hands. She looked down at him, dropping the hammer suddenly and jumping back as if in shock. Her hand shook as she raised it to cover her mouth, then, upon seeing her own bloody fingers, she cast it away from her face.

"What did you do? Why would you—" I asked, falling to my knees next to the body in shock. "Why did you—" I didn't know where to start as I tried to process all that had happened.

"Ryan, I… I had to…" she whispered from behind me.

Maybe she did.

"He was going to kill us…"

Maybe he was.

"I had no choice…"

That might be true.

"I'm sorry…"

At her words, I felt the knife slide from the back pocket of my jeans. "What are you—"

I didn't get to finish the question. Didn't get to see her face.

Instead, I felt something cold slice into my back. At first, in one blissfully unaware moment, I thought someone was pouring ice over my skin, and I tried to look around. But then I realized what was happening. I knew the sting of freezing cold metal, understood what was happening as I felt it tearing through my muscles. Someone was stabbing me with the knife. I felt the blade tear through my skin again. Near my spine. Into my side.

Again.

Again.

Again.

I screamed—or, at least, thought of screaming—as I fell on top of the man's body. What had happened? What had Grace done? The questions swam in my mind as my vision grew blurry, his warm, wet blood spreading out on the floor underneath my head.

As the world grew dark, I heard the *click, clack* of her shoes on the floor as she walked away from me.

Steady.

Not in a hurry.

Not trying to save me.

Why wouldn't Grace try to save me?

Why had she tried to kill me?

The answers didn't come, and as I tried to force them, the thoughts formed less and less. They stopped making sense. No thoughts. No words.

Just buzzing in my ears.

Ringing.

Silence.

My eyes closed again, and it was a struggle to keep them open. So, I didn't.

I didn't fight.

Couldn't.

My eyes stayed closed, the silence surrounding me with strange comfort and peace.

Nothing.

Nothing.

Nothing.

Was this death?

I welcomed the darkness.

PART TWO

CHAPTER TWENTY

Janie

Twenty Years Ago

When we pulled up to the cabin, the gravel crunching under our tires and trees covered in changing leaves rustling in the wind, I tried to hide my excitement. It was the first vacation we'd ever taken as a family.

Well, the first vacation that I could remember, at least. Mom said there was a time once before, when I was very young, when we'd gone to the beach in Florida for a whole week. I couldn't remember it and she had no pictures to prove it, so it didn't count for me.

Not that that was unusual, mind you. The 'no pictures' thing.

In fact, it was very much the usual.

What pictures and sentimental things we'd once had, were destroyed one by one any time Dad got mad. I'd long since learned not to bring home anything important to me from school.

The car rolled to a stop, and I waited for Dad to get out. He opened my door—thanks to the child locks, even at fifteen, I wasn't able to open them myself. Too afraid I'd run or signal for help. It was why my windows were tinted as dark as he could have them done.

But this was different. A vacation. An escape from the only four walls I'd ever spent the night in. Aside from my school, the only place I'd ever spent more than just a few minutes inside.

Even Mom, who was usually quiet and subdued, seemed happier. I stepped out, my body tingling with excitement as my feet hit the gravel. The place was spectacular. Even better than what I'd imagined.

It was a *real* cabin, like I'd only seen in storybooks and on TV. Wooden with tall windows and thick beams. It had been built into the earth, a steep cliff off the side of the driveway that led to thick woods all around us.

"Keep up," Dad called over his shoulder when he realized I wasn't behind him. Our bags were lying beside the car, and I knew I was the one who'd be required to carry them. My parents were already on the small porch, and as I struggled to carry the three bags, Dad turned a combination lock on a small grab box near the door, which opened to reveal a key. He pulled it out and stuck it into the doorknob, letting us inside.

"Set those there," he grunted, pointing to the small table to my left. I did as he said, looking around at the view. It was incredible. Somehow, when he'd said we were going on vacation, I believed there had to be a catch. Or that he was lying altogether. I held onto hope, but only slightly. In this family, there wasn't much use for anything that resembled hope. It was a lot like love—something reserved for TV and books. A fairytale. As fictitious as magic wands and pirate ships.

I walked forward, toward the wall made entirely of glass. It was the closest thing I'd ever seen to something you could describe as magical. The sun reflected off the shiny coat of protectant on the wood decking outside, tiny specks of dust floating up into the beams. I couldn't seem to keep my jaw closed as I took it in.

This place is amazing. I thought it over and over, never allowing myself to speak it aloud. If I did, if he saw me enjoying myself too much, I was sure he'd find a way to take it away from me. Maybe he'd make me spend the whole week in the car—it wouldn't be the first time.

Somehow, speaking any sort of joy or happiness out loud always managed to ensure the source of said happiness would disappear. So instead, I chose to spend most of my life, experience most of my emotions, inside my head. It was where I was safest. Where no one could hurt me but myself.

"Brenda, pick out which room we want. She can have the other." I spun around to face my parents, watching as my mom walked across the living room and peered inside the bedroom to my right. She gave a small smile.

"This one's fine, Cal."

"Fine?" he grumbled, sticking his own head in the room. I suspected, like myself, Mom was worried about seeming to like it too much, for fear he'd choose the other one out of sheer spite. He looked around, his upper lip curled as if it wasn't the nicest place he'd ever set foot in, then shoved past her, nearly knocking her over on his way across the room toward the other bedroom.

He did the same in it, stuck his head inside and glanced around, nodding slowly. "This one's nicer. She can have that one." He looked down the set of stairs to his right. "Game room's downstairs."

My father spoke mostly in grunts and mostly to himself. It was something we were all used to. I watched him descend the stairs before I heard Mom's gruff voice.

"What are you waiting for? Get the bags in the rooms before your father gets upset." She pointed her long, bony finger across the room toward the table.

I nodded, hurrying toward the bags at her instructions.

"Get down here, Brenda." I heard my father's voice from downstairs and watched as Mom trembled, jumping to answer his call.

"Coming," she called. She scurried across the room, running her hands along the wall as she made her way down the stairs.

I breathed a sigh of relief, grateful for the break from them. I'd spent two hours in the car, hoping not to breathe the wrong way or make the wrong face. Anything that might upset him. As excited as I was to be somewhere new, to experience something different, I couldn't help feeling vulnerable, too. At home, I knew where to hide when things got bad. I could stay out of sight. Stay hidden and safe—or as safe as was possible with my parents.

But in the car, I was exposed. I'd thought once we'd arrived, I might feel better. But in that moment, I realized, even here in this beautiful, magical place, I was still exposed. I felt my excitement dissipating.

Any shred of warmth I'd felt just moments ago was washed away as I remembered I was supposed to be doing something. I took my parents' bags into the bedroom my father had claimed was 'better' and placed them on the end of the queen-sized bed, noting the Jacuzzi tub in the far corner.

Then, I went across the living room and into the room that was mine, surprised to find it was a mirror image of the first room. Jacuzzi tub in the corner, private bathroom with stand-in shower, and TV mounted on the wall. I placed my bag on the dresser and bounced on the bed. It was the most comfortable piece of furniture I'd ever had the pleasure of resting on. In fact, I would've been perfectly happy to spend the rest of my vacation right there. If I was allowed to, I'd do just that.

Of course, it was never that easy.

"Hey!" my father bellowed, his voice practically shaking the house as it tore through the silence. I jumped up like I'd been caught doing something awful, my ears burning red from embarrassment.

What did I do? I tried to think quickly. The bags were in the right place… unless he'd wanted me to unpack them. He hadn't specified, but maybe I was supposed to know. If that was the case, I was sure to get it.

I walked out of the bedroom, squeezing my hands into fists to hide the shaking. I sucked in a deep breath, letting it out methodically.

I could never let my guard down. Never believe I was safe. Never be foolish enough to think I was allowed to be happy.

My parents weren't upstairs yet, so the issue wasn't the bags. Instead, I followed their hushed voices down the stairs. There was no railing, which seemed to be an accident waiting to happen, but I ran my hands along the wall to keep steady.

The bottom floor, like the top, had an exterior wall made entirely of glass. There was a pool table in the center of the room and two loveseats that appeared to be brand new. There was a heaviness in the air down there. Dank and heavy, as if there was no airflow in that part of the house at all. Straight ahead, there was a closed door, and another door that was opened, giving way to a dark bathroom.

"You'll sleep down here. Give your mother and me some privacy," came the order.

I looked at the loveseats again. They were small, half my length, and though they looked comfortable, they were nothing compared to the bed upstairs. Add that to the fact that there was no TV, Jacuzzi tub, and apparently no air conditioning, and I struggled to hide my disappointment.

"You hear me?"

I nodded. "Yes, sir."

"You don't need all that space anyway. It'll just spoil you."

"Yes, sir." I turned to head back up the stairs and collect my bag.

"Where do you think you're going?" Dad asked.

"To get my bag," I said, but judging by the sneer on Dad's face, that was the wrong answer.

"Leave it. I don't want to be trippin' over it when I need to get from place to place. There's nowhere to store it down here. You'll just have to go back and forth when you need something."

Again, I nodded. That was my father—cruel just for the sake of being cruel. The room was good enough to keep my stuff in, but too good for me to sleep in. "Okay."

"This place is supposed to be stocked with enough food to last us the week." He patted Mom's butt. "What do you say we have dinner on the deck?"

Mom nodded, but the excitement in her voice didn't match her tired expression. "That sounds great." She looked at me out the corner of her eye, obviously wanting me to leave them alone. Dad hadn't dismissed me yet, though, so it was a tightrope of decisions—what was right and what was wrong.

"What are you waiting for? Go find something to make us for dinner," Dad growled, ending my internal war to find the right answer. "If there's enough, you can have some of it, too."

Without waiting for him to say more, I scurried up the staircase, through the living room, and into the kitchen. The freezer was small, but like Dad had said, it was filled with food—mostly meat. There was more food there than we could've eaten in a month if we tried.

I pulled out a pack of ground hamburger. There were plenty of things I wanted to try, but this was what I was most comfortable with. It wasn't like I'd ever cooked a steak or salmon before. Burger was a luxury in our house, and more often than not, our dinners consisted of a combination peanut butter sandwiches, beans, plain noodles, and soups that could be extremely watered down. If I tried to make something like steaks and ended up ruining it, I'd be in for the beating of a lifetime. No, unless Dad said differently, I had to stick with things I knew I could do well.

I turned on the hot water, waiting until it scalded my fingers to place the burger underneath it. I opened the cabinet while the meat thawed, noticing that there was not only bread there waiting for us, but they had real, *actual* hamburger buns.

I pulled the package out, wanting to taste one just for the sake of it, my mouth practically watering with the thought. I grabbed a box of macaroni and a can of green beans. It was actually a decent meal, if I did say so myself.

And, of course, I *would* be the only one to say so.

While I prepared the meal, Mom and Dad made their way up the stairs and onto the deck. I could hear them out there, laughing and carrying on—mostly Dad, but Mom joined in sometimes when, I assumed, she felt safe enough to do so.

I was forgotten, blending in with the wallpaper of their lives, only existing to bring them things and cook their meals. It sounded sad, I guess, but honestly it was okay with me. I preferred it that way. When I was seen, I could be hurt. I could do something wrong.

As long as I remained invisible, I didn't have as much to fear.

When the door opened, it took all I had for me not to jump. I heard his footsteps headed my direction, but I didn't look back, pretending to busy myself by staring at the meat as it sizzled, running my spatula over the grooves of it, the savory smell filling my nostrils.

He opened the refrigerator, and I sucked in a deep breath. Maybe he wouldn't acknowledge me at all.

"Almost done?"

I swallowed. "J-just about."

"Good. Don't keep me waiting." With that, he slammed the refrigerator shut, and I heard the beer bottles in his hands clinking together as he made his way back outside.

I had no idea why my father had brought us here. Aside from the vacation in Florida that Mom talked about, we'd never done anything that remotely resembled a vacation, and he wasn't the type to do anything just for the fun of it. He'd never even brought up vacationing as far as I could remember. Did he just need to get away? Was he celebrating some big news at work? The torment of wondering why we were here while trying to balance happiness enough to seem appreciative and fear that I'd look *too* happy had my mind spinning.

He'd come home from work a few days ago and told me to pack our bags. He hadn't said where we were going until the day before we left, and even then, he'd just called it a cabin in the mountains. I didn't know if we were going to the nearby mountains or mountains far away, and when I'd had the chance to ask Mom, she didn't either. I was supposed to be in school, so I wondered how long we'd be gone. But neither of us knew. He hadn't told us what we were traveling for and, of course, we couldn't ask. All we could do was wait. Wait for him to volunteer the information, or else we'd never know at all.

When the food was ready, I pulled three gray, ceramic plates from the cabinet and prepared them, giving us each a hefty portion of everything. I made Dad's noticeably bigger, because I knew if I didn't, there was a good chance he'd say something about it. I didn't want to take any chances. If there was anything I could do to keep this vacation peaceful, I would do it.

I lifted their plates, carrying them across the living room carefully. When I reached the door, I tried to decide how I would open it with both hands full. Dad watched me but made no move to help.

Finally, I walked back into the kitchen and set one of the plates down, carrying his outside first. I placed it on the glass patio table in front of him.

"'Bout time," he grumbled, reaching over me to take the burger from his plate before I'd moved my hands. "Don't keep your mother waitin'." He spoke with his mouth full, chunks of burger flying from his lips.

I nodded, turning around as quickly as possible in order to escape. In record time, I had Mom's plate in front of her before bringing my own out and sitting between them. I ate slowly, cautiously, the silence weighing on me.

Why weren't they talking?

What was going on?

"Well, I guess we should tell her the good news," Dad said as he wiped his mouth with the back of his hand before letting out a loud belch. I glanced at his empty plate, then at him. His mouth was twisted into a fierce grin, his eyes locked on Mom.

I looked across the table at her, surprised to see she was smiling, too. She rested her fork across her plate, looking down at her lap as one hand slid under the table to cradle her stomach.

No.

"We're going to have a baby, Janie." Her face was flushed red.

No. Not again.

There had been one other—a baby that had been spared a life like mine. I was just ten at the time, but I remembered this feeling. The dread, the fear…

*

Mom was halfway through her pregnancy when he'd come home and kicked her in the stomach. She'd started bleeding within the hour.

The next day, she went into labor at home while Dad was at work. I wanted to call him, knowing he'd be mad if I didn't, but she insisted that we couldn't bother him. So, I sat by her side while she screamed and squirmed and bled and sweated, each hour that passed bringing us closer to when he'd come home and discover our secret.

That's what it felt like, too. A dirty, little secret between the two of us. Like if she could just hurry up and have the thing, we could hide it away and pretend it never happened. Instead, it took hours for the pains to start coming closer together. I'd read books throughout her pregnancy to try and find out what to expect, but there were no books on labor in my school's library and very few with pregnant people at all. A few of my teachers had had babies, and some had even been pregnant while I was in their class, but it wasn't like they talked about the process. I knew from some of the other girls in my grade that there was a lot of screaming, a lot of blood, and sometimes even poop involved.

I didn't want to deal with any of it, honestly, but she needed me. So, I held her hand, and we waited. It was taking forever, though.

When he finally did get home, I spoke up. Said I thought we should get her to the doctor. That got me a smack across the face. Dad didn't trust doctors. He didn't trust anyone.

The baby was born that night. A little girl. I remember staring at her tiny body on the comforter in between Mom's legs. The baby was so small she fit into my palm. Mom didn't want to hold her, so I did. Just for a second. Long enough to see she wasn't alive. She didn't cry, didn't breathe even once.

There'd been so much pain for something so small. Mom bled a lot afterward. I didn't think it was possible to bleed as much as she had, but I was very wrong. She bled so much that I thought she was going to die. The thought was terrifying. Mom wasn't great, but at least she rarely hit me. Almost never sent me to bed without supper. If she was gone, I'd be left with Dad, and I was sure things would get worse for me...

*

I made a plan then—if Mom died, I'd run. I didn't care that I had nowhere to go, no money, no family. I'd run until I couldn't anymore. I'd heard about girls that lived on the streets at school, the things they did to make money, the way they scraped by. I was scrappy. I knew how to run a house, cook a meal. I could find a job somewhere—I'd be sixteen soon.

But even if I had to do the other things, the sexual things I'd heard about, the things Mom did with Dad sometimes, I was sure that was preferable to this. Foster care wasn't an option. Even if I managed to get Dad turned in, he'd find me. And no one wanted teenagers anyway. Running was the only chance I stood.

*

I lay in bed that night with Mom. She never did touch the baby, even after I had—just shivered and cried all night. When we woke up, it was gone.

*

I had no idea what he did with it, but I assumed it was buried in the backyard with the dog I once loved too much.

Since then, there had been no talk of the baby, or of having another. At one point, Mom asked me to bring her birth control, so I'd gone to the free clinic and done just that. Eventually, Dad found the packs and beat us both for them.

That was two years ago.

Now, as I stared across the table at them, I only felt anger. How could they have let this happen? *How could she?*

I wasn't foolish enough to believe that she had any choice in the sex—Dad wasn't the type to ask for anything. But why had she told him she was pregnant in the first place? Why hadn't she gotten an abortion? Bringing a baby into this situation, if she even managed to carry to term, would only bring devastation.

"Well, don't look so disappointed," my mom said, shaking her head. "You're gonna be running off and leaving us soon enough. We aren't ready for an empty house just yet." She winked at me, and I felt the bile rising in my throat.

That's what this is about? In just over two years, I'd be old enough to leave and they'd be on their own. Expected to wash their own clothes, prepare their own meals, and clean their own toilets. But now—now they'd be raising a new child to do just that. How soon would they expect it to be done? A toddler would need someone to take care of them, not the other way around.

Of course, by age five, I'd been taking care of them more than they'd ever taken care of me. I put my hand to my own stomach, sure I was going to be sick.

A heavy hand slammed into the back of my head, bringing me back to reality. My skin stung from the force.

"Tell your momma congratulations," he ordered.

I blinked back tears, nodding. "C-congratulations, Mom. That's really good news."

"You don't seem happy about it," Dad said matter-of-factly.

When I glanced his way, he was wearing an undeniable smirk. Was he trying to rile me up? It wasn't going to work. "I am," I insisted. "Real happy. I'm just feeling tired."

"Tired," he scoffed. "That's what's wrong with your generation. You don't know a damn thing about hard work. Take me for example: got a job at the factory when I was younger than you, worked my way all the way up to a foreman's job by twenty-two. What will you have done by twenty-two? Nothing, no doubt. You'll be as useless as the day you were born." He took a swig of his beer.

I wasn't sure what to say. It wasn't, by any stretch of the imagination, unusual for him to pick me apart and tear me down. It was just an average day, but the news had caught me off guard, and I wasn't thinking straight. When I felt cool tears gathering in my eyes, I looked down, blinking rapidly in hopes of drying them before he saw.

"What's the matter, snowflake? Suddenly you have nothing to say? Can't defend your laziness?"

I sniffed, looking back up. I'd long since given up on the idea of Mom ever defending me. When he came for me, I was on my own.

"You're right," I said. "I'm lazy. I need to do better. Do you... do you think I should find a job?" The idea was delightful. Any time I could spend outside our house was a saving grace. If I could get a job, things wouldn't be as tight financially, I'd be able to spend time away from my parents, and I might even be able to hide some money away for when I turned eighteen.

He locked his jaw, obviously taken aback by the suggestion. His upper lip curled into a snarl. "Nah, nobody'd want ya anyway." With that, he drained the last of his beer. "And even if they did, they'd let ya work 'til you were old and stiff, and then they'd let you go to bring on some young buck half your age." His eyes were dark then—colder than usual—as reality slammed into my chest.

He lost his job.

He'd lost the job that put food on the table, no matter how small the portions, and kept him away from us for ten hours a day, five days a week. A sudden sense of hopelessness overwhelmed me, and I felt new tears in my eyes.

I looked to Mom, who was staring at her hands in her lap. Had she known? Why were we here spending money on a vacation we obviously didn't have anymore? We should've been saving.

"I'm sorry, Dad," I whispered, unsure what to say.

"I don't need your pity. Either of you." He stood from the table, leaving his plate for me to clean up as he stormed away. "Now, finish eating and get this shit cleaned up."

With that, he was back in the house, and we were left alone.

Mom sighed dramatically. "Now look what you've done. You've gone and upset your father when he was just trying to do something nice for us."

"What was he trying to do, Mom? Why are we here? If Dad lost his job, how can we afford to be here?" She twisted her lips when I looked up at her, refusing to meet my eyes. *"Mom?"*

"Oh, fine. Well, if you must know, we aren't exactly paying to stay here." She scoffed, her hands shaking as she reached for the bottle of beer beside her plate.

"Should you be drinking that?"

"I'm the parent here," she snipped, taking another drink. "Your father's in a mood. He's trying to hide it, but I'll need this to deal with him later, trust me."

I sighed, changing the subject. "What do you mean we aren't paying to stay here?"

"It's none of your business, Janie. And if your dad wants you to know what's going on, he'll tell you. Just eat your food before he comes back out here and takes it away." She took a bite of her macaroni with a trembling hand.

I lowered my voice, struck by her words. "Mom, what's going on? Is Dad in trouble? Are we hiding out?"

She rolled her eyes, scoffing. "Of course, we aren't 'hiding out.'"

"Then what?"

She sighed. "Well, if you must know—she used her fork to scoot around her food, speaking slowly as she avoided eye contact with me—"this place belongs to your dad's old boss. Some rich phony baloney. He rents it out to pay for his wife's plastic surgery." She gestured toward her chest. "A guy your dad works—*worked*—with had it rented for this week, but something came up. Your dad is supposed to be paying him back on Monday." She snorted.

"And what are we doing here?"

"Just celebrating. Getting what we deserve," she said with an indignant smile. "What do you think?"

I shook my head. It didn't make any sense, but that wasn't unusual for my parents. For all I knew, she was lying anyway. Again, I lowered my voice, leaning in closer to her. "Mom, you know I can take you to get an abortion, don't you? You don't have to do this. One of the girls in my class—"

THWACK. The slap came out of nowhere, stopping me mid-sentence. Her eyes were wide, face pink with anger. "Don't you *dare* talk to me about that. If your dad even heard so much as a whisper—"

"He doesn't have to know…" I rubbed my cheek. "It's still early enough."

I saw the distress in her eyes as she shook her head again. "I said no, Janie. And don't ever ask me again. Your father would kill us both." With that, she abandoned her food, standing up from the table and making her way inside.

I was left alone, with no appetite to speak of and a deep well of terror in my chest.

CHAPTER TWENTY-ONE

Janie

That night, after I'd cleaned up dinner and done the dishes, I spent a few minutes in the bathroom cleaning the deep gash in my side from a beating last week. It was red and inflamed, probably infected. I opened the cabinet under the sink, hoping there might be something there to disinfect it, but there was nothing except spare rolls of toilet paper. I grabbed a washcloth and cleaned it with water, despite the pain.

When I was finished, I retreated out to the bedroom where my bag was still resting on the bed and unzipped it, sliding my clothes out of the way. Near the bottom of the suitcase were three library books I'd checked out before we'd left for vacation. The first, a ratty copy of a Lois Duncan novel called *They Never Came Home*, had a dog-eared page where I last left off. I took the book and headed out of the bedroom and across the living room, walking as quickly as possible past where my parents sat on the couch.

To my relief, neither said anything to me as I headed down the stairs. I sank into the small loveseat on the first floor next to the pool table, opening up the book and trying to lose myself in a world that was so unlike my own. In the stories I read, there was almost always a happy ending. Even in the darker ones, if you looked closely enough, there was a reason to hope. The characters had someone to care about them. I wondered why I couldn't be so lucky. What had I done so wrong that I had been chosen to lead the life I did? I thought about the girls I went to school with, the pretty ones with the new clothes and braces to fix their bright, white teeth. The ones with the newest, latest things and the best cars and the sweetest boyfriends.

Then there was me.

Why did I have to be different?

Everyone hated me: my parents, my friends, myself. But why? What had I done to deserve it? Was there anything anyone could do to deserve such horrible things?

I reread the page I was on, having not paid attention as I went through it the first time. That was when I heard the first sign of trouble.

"What? You think he's good lookin' or somethin'?" Dad demanded, his voice a loud roar.

I didn't hear Mom's answer, her voice barely audible from where I was.

"Oh, no. I know damn well what you meant." I winced as I heard his boots hit the floor above my head when he stood. "Do you think I'm stupid?"

"No," came the squeal, and I heard the first thud.

I knew better than to intervene. It didn't help; it only made things worse for the both of us. I squeezed my eyes shut and opened them wide again, staring at the page with intense focus as I tried to tune them out.

"You think he'd ever want you, you stupid bitch?" he demanded, his voice growing louder. "He's a fuckin' millionaire, with supermodels at his beck and call. He sure don't want your dumb, pregnant ass." He growled, and I heard the next smack loud and clear.

"I didn't mean anything by it," she whined. "I swear I didn't. He's just a good actor, but ugly as they come, I swear." She was trying to justify whatever it was that she'd said, but we both knew it would only make things worse.

I flipped the page, though I hadn't read what the last one said. Things were quiet upstairs for a moment, and I hoped the fight had ended before it truly began. Before I could get too calm, I heard a loud *THUNK,* then the undeniable sound of glass breaking. Mom began to cry.

He'd thrown her into the wall, knocked some dishes off the counter. It hadn't taken long for me to learn the sounds of their fighting. I knew the different sounds they'd make—could discern a punch from a kick, a slap from the pulling of her hair, an arm twist from him stepping on her hand, a slam against the wall from a shove to the floor. I'd become an expert in my own hell.

I knew from the lilts of his voice at dinner whether we'd have a quiet night or a loud one. It was like Mom had said at dinner. He was in a mood. Always in a mood. And we were tools at his disposal to work through said moods.

I jumped to attention as I heard his heavy footsteps coming down the stairs, closing my book and hiding it behind my back. I couldn't count the number of library books he'd destroyed, that I'd had to work hours shelving books to pay off. I'd been restricted to only checking out the books that were in less than great condition. Luckily for me, most of my favorite books were popular enough to be in bad shape.

He opened the bathroom door and pulled open the cabinet under the sink. As if he hadn't been expecting me to be there, when I moved, he jumped. His eyes narrowed at me. "The hell are you staring at?"

I shook my head, pretending I hadn't heard anything that had happened. "C-can I help you find something?"

"What are you hiding behind your back?"

The blood drained from my face. "Nothing." There was no use lying. "Just a library book."

"Bring it here," he demanded, holding out his hand.

Now I'd never know how it ended.

I walked forward cautiously, tears pricking my eyes as I laid the book in his palm. He looked at it, curling his lip in disgust. "Well, that's fitting." He tucked it into his back pocket. "Now, help me find the bleach!" he cried, slamming his hand on the counter. "Your mom got blood all over upstairs. I need to clean it. Get over here and find it while I look for towels."

I took a step past him, bending down beside where he had been as I searched for the bleach. I tried not to think about my mother upstairs, bleeding and hurt. Would it be her head this time? Her face? I'd stitched and bandaged up more parts of her body than I could count.

"There's this cleaner," I said, reaching for the spray can of bathroom cleaner. "It says it has bleach in it."

He bent down next to me, his hand on my back. I tensed, sucking in a breath I couldn't bring myself to release. When he reached for the bottle, his lips grew near my ear, and he whispered the words that would haunt me the rest of my life.

I could kill her, you know?

CHAPTER TWENTY-TWO

Janie

I didn't dare look at him, too shaken by his words to comment. He was expecting a rise out of me, a reaction, but I couldn't give it. I was petrified—unable to move or think or breathe.

"See, there's a reason I picked this place," he went on. Once he had an audience for his madness, he rarely stopped.

I stared at the lines of bottles of cleaner in front of me, taking in the pictures of happy pets and smiling sponges.

"A little while ago, a woman was killed here. Buried right out back, they say." His nails dug into the skin of my back. "The way I figure it, people won't be asking too many questions if it happens again." He pressed his lips further onto my ear. "But even if they do, we could be long gone."

"W-we?" I asked, my voice a quiet squeak.

"We could get away from here. Away from *her*."

"W-why? What's she done? What about the b-baby?" I asked, trying to focus, to think. I needed to do something, but what? How could I protect her when it would surely mean I would die, too?

He scoffed. "Your mom ain't thinkin' about what a baby will mean for us. How are we gonna raise it? How are we gonna be able to afford it? She won't get a job. I can't just keep carryin' all of us—"

"I'll get a job," I offered. "I swear I will. I can do this for us all."

He patted my back again, so hard it stung, but I didn't dare let it show. "Nah, I'm handling it. I'll figure it out. Always have. Now, get outside for a while. Let me handle everything. And if ya say anything to your momma, I'll kill her for sure. Then I'll kill you."

I knew it was a risk, but I had to bring it up. Had to argue. Though I didn't know if he was serious, I couldn't let him even consider it. "You don't have to do that. We'll figure it out together. There are options, Dad. She doesn't have to have the baby—"

Before I could finish the sentence, he slammed my head into the counter, and I lost my balance, closing my eyes as the familiar ringing in my ears came back. "We ain't no baby killers," he growled.

"Cal?" my mom's soft voice called. She rounded the corner, and I gasped as I saw the blood running down the front of her arm. For half a second, I thought she'd tried to cut her wrists. Then, I saw the glass sticking out of her skin.

My dad jumped up, rushing toward her with a towel and the bleach cleaner. Without warning or hesitation, he ripped the two large shards of glass from the wounds and tossed them to the ground, then wiped across her arm with the towel as she winced in pain, her eyes bloodshot and tear-filled.

"Here. Hold still." He sprayed the cleaner directly on her wound, despite her whimpering protests. "I said hold still." He dug his grip into her skin until there were glowing white halos around each of his fingers. When he was done, he wrapped the towel around her arm and tucked it into her chest. He held her tight, her wounded arm squeezed between them in a hug. I saw the confusion in her face, his words ringing in my ears.

I needed to warn her, but I had no idea how. It wasn't the first time we'd been threatened with death, but somehow this felt more real. Was he going to do it soon? How long were we going to be staying here? I had to get Mom alone so I could tell her what he'd said. "Maybe I could help get it cleaned up? It'll need to be bandaged."

"It doesn't matter," Dad said gruffly. "I told you to get outside."

"But it's dark—there could be wolves." I would've preferred wolves to him, but I had to fight for her. Even if she'd never fought for me. Even when she'd blamed me for every horrible thing he'd ever done to me. Even if she'd never tried to get us away. I wasn't her, and I wouldn't let myself become who she was.

"Your father said get outside, Janie," Mom said sharply.

"But—"

"Go!" Dad bellowed.

I studied her eyes, an unexpected hint of dread in them. Something that went deeper than the usual fight. To this day, I have to wonder if she knew. If she knew what was coming when she came down those stairs, when she climbed in the car. If she knew that the dinner I prepared would be her last.

Some part of me thinks she must have. As I walked past her, she reached for my arm, squeezing it gently with her unwounded hand.

"Momma…" I couldn't stop the tears from falling then.

Her face was as still as stone. "Go, Janie. I'll be fine." She held my eyes a bit longer than usual before looking back at my father. "Your father and I want to be alone."

With that, I took a step toward the door, refusing to look back. Walking away that night would haunt me for the rest of my life, but I had to do it. *I had to.*

As I walked down the hill and out into the woods, I turned around, shielded just far enough that I couldn't be seen, but I could still see them. I had the strangest thought occur to me then. Death has a smell—strange and ineffable. Primal. Like birth. Like the smell of the baby when it was born. Like the smell of a room filled with grief, of tears, of hopelessness. Somehow, as I stared up into the windows of the house that night, the glowing amber beams from beyond the glass, I knew I would smell it again.

I knew what was coming before it did.

I can't explain it. It doesn't make any sense, even now, how I knew. He'd lied before. He'd threatened to kill us both countless times. But there it was. A niggle in my brain.

She's going to die.

He's going to kill her.

For real this time.

I was going to smell death again.

I watched in absolute, chilling horror as he led her up the staircase toward the second floor. It was where it would happen. Somehow, I knew. It was where it had happened before. Had it been him? Before? The other woman? Or was that all a lie, too? Did the cabin even belong to his boss? Or had that been what he'd told Mom to get her there? I didn't know, and I suspected I never would.

I should've moved, should've done something. But what was there to do? I watched him take her hand, sliding it up over her arm. She stumbled. Had she been drinking? More than the beer at dinner? It wasn't unlikely. My mom had always been a drinker; I think it was the only way she could tolerate being around him. Maybe it was what she needed to numb the pain of her existence.

When he spun her around, his back to the window, I saw the blade. Right next to my book in his back pocket. *No.* Even from where I was, hidden in the vast darkness of the forest, it was there. Obvious. Deadly.

Once he pulled it from his belt, it was over. I should've never left them alone. I'd wanted to doubt his words, but I shouldn't have. By the time I accepted that, I had no chance of saving her. I moved forward, out of the safety of the trees and shadows, pushing myself to move faster despite the fact that my legs were begging me to slow down.

My joints ached, my ankle throbbing from a recent sprain, and I knew the wound on my side had ripped open. The partially healed gash from the steel toe of his boot. It hadn't healed well anyway. I'd only cleaned it with water, using bits of a shirt I'd torn up to tie around my waist until it stopped bleeding, and now it was more infected than ever. I needed to see a doctor, but that didn't matter. I never would. It would heal on its own or I would die, like every other wound I'd ever suffered.

Forgetting my own pain, I glanced back up at the window, and I saw the knife in Dad's hand.

I was too late.

He held it above her, more for show than anything. She didn't move—frozen in fear. I didn't either. Couldn't.

My breath caught in my chest as I tried to decide what to do. What could I do? She didn't move as he lowered the blade to her chest, but I heard her scream. It cut through the glass, through the silence of the forest, sending chills across my filthy arms. Birds flew out of trees at the disturbance, the sound piercing through the night.

He lifted the blade again, bringing it to her stomach as she fell backward with a solid swipe. With this blow, she crumpled, and the horror in my chest exploded, cold spreading to every part of my extremities.

She was dead. My mom was dead.

He dropped the knife, taking a half-step back and looking over what he had done. He rubbed his hand over his lips and shook his head. He lifted a foot to her, kicking her hip. When she didn't move, he bent down. For just a moment, I thought he was going to attend to her.

Instead, he picked up the knife, wiped it off on his shirt, and slid it back into his belt. When he stood, he kicked her again, and I felt my stomach begin to rumble. I was going to be sick, but I hadn't eaten much in days and hadn't been able to finish dinner. What could I possibly still be retaining?

When I looked up, he was gone from the window, though her body still lay there. I rolled my eyes at the thought—*where else would it go?*

Then, panic jolted through me as I looked back up to where he'd been standing. Could he see me from where I was? In the light from the porch, it was possible. I was no longer hidden.

Could he be coming for me next?

To kill me or take me with him? Killing would've been preferable.

I didn't have time to think.

I had to act.

And so, I ran.

I ran for the house without thought. This would be my end, or it would be his. I would make him pay for what he'd done. To her, to me...

I shoved in the door and bounded up the stairs. There was the smell again—just as I remembered it.

Death.

I wasn't sure how to feel about it. On one hand, I loved my mother as much as I was capable of loving another person. By that, I supposed I just didn't want her to die. Seeing her lying there, her chest neither rising nor falling, the wounds still bleeding onto the hardwood, it didn't bring me any sort of pleasure like it would've if it were him.

Dad was standing next to her body, almost as if he were in a trance, the knife sticking out from the back of his belt.

He knew I was behind him, but he didn't bother to turn in my direction. He underestimated me. Underestimated my fury.

"It's done," he whispered. "It's just you and me now." I was silent as I stood behind him. "I need you to find a shovel. We'll bury her out back, real deep, clean up this mess, and then we'll go. By the time they find her, we'll be long gone."

Lifting my hand slowly and carefully, I reached for the knife. I slid it gently from his belt, easing it out so he wouldn't notice the disturbance.

"It had to be done," he said, but I wasn't sure who he was trying to convince. "She was weighing us down."

I nodded, though he still couldn't see me, and I gave the knife one final tug. I would take his life as he had hers. Before I could convince myself to do it, he realized what I was doing and spun around.

"What the—" Seeing the knife in my hand, he lunged toward me, his hand outstretched. I shoved the blade upward with every bit of my strength, the steel of the blade connecting with the soft tissue of his neck. He jerked back, pulling the knife with him. I stumbled, reaching for it, half in shock at the sight of the blood spurting from his neck.

I grabbed it again, slicing at his neck as he fell. His body landed next to Mom's, flopping and gurgling as he fought to speak, no doubt telling me he was going to catch and kill me.

But he didn't.

Couldn't.

He couldn't move. I'd made sure of it.

His blood poured out of his body, mixing with Mom's on the floor. With one last look at what I'd done, I dropped the knife and ran, heading straight for the front door.

Once I hit the driveway, I headed for the woods. I had to keep going, despite my pounding heart and shaking legs. I could never stop.

I'd killed my father. Perhaps people would believe I'd killed my mother, too. How would I explain that they were wrong? How would I prove it?

I had no proof. I was the sole survivor, the only witness or suspect.

I had done a horrible thing, and I deserved to pay for it.

But I'd rather pay for it a thousand times over than to ever have to set foot in a house with that man again.

At that thought, I smiled.

Despite everything that had happened, the blood drying on my face and the vision of his last breath in my head, I smiled.

CHAPTER TWENTY-THREE

Janie

I don't know how long I'd been walking when the officer found me. It felt like a long, endless tunnel of days. I was sure I'd fallen asleep at some point, but I never stopped moving. I was in and out of consciousness, in and out of awareness. Nothing made sense, and yet, everything was crystal clear.

When I saw the flashing red and blue lights in the darkness, my first instinct was to run, but I knew it was no use. I had to think quickly. I was dirty, covered in blood, and frightened. Was I going to jail? Or… juvie? Was I old enough to be tried as an adult?

I didn't know.

So, when the police cruiser slowed to a stop directly in front of me, my body illuminated by the bright headlights, I knew I had one chance to get it right.

And, just like that, my father's words were in my head. His story about the other woman who'd died.

I knew what to do. I just had to hope it worked.

Two officers exited the vehicle, a man and a woman—for a brief second, I pretended it was Mom and Dad and that they'd come to get me, to pretend it was all a prank, but I knew that wasn't the case.

The female officer approached me first, her hands out in front of her cautiously as she eased toward me. She was speaking, but piecing together what she was saying took extra focus.

"Sweetie, can you hear me? Are you hurt?"

I shook my head, my voice caught in my throat as I tried to answer. Hurt how? Physically, not really, though the pain in my side begged to differ. But I'd never be the same, and that felt like it hurt somehow.

I felt different. Diminished. Like a huge part of who I was had died on the floor with my parents. And that realization did hurt. The Janie who walked into that cabin just hours ago didn't exist anymore. She wouldn't ever again.

"Is that your blood? Or... someone else's?" the male officer asked, standing behind the woman.

"I... no, it's not mine." I couldn't meet their eyes, keeping my gaze locked on the ground.

"Can you tell us what happened? Are you in danger?"

I shook my head—slowly, sadly. "No."

The male officer spoke into the radio on his shoulder then, but I wasn't paying attention. Numbers, a direction, an address... He called for backup while I waited in silence. "We're going to get you some help, okay?" he said, when he was done.

"Where are your parents, sweetie?" the woman asked. "Can you tell me? Do you know?"

I was silent, twisting my bare toes on the pavement. I hadn't realized how bloody they were until that moment. My run through the woods had taken a serious toll on them. Why hadn't I felt the pain?

"I have a daughter who is about your age, and I know if she were lost, I'd be worried sick." She paused. "Your folks must be worried about you. Do they know where you are? Do they know you're out here?"

Again, I didn't answer.

"What's your name?" she pressed on.

"Janie Foreman," I whispered, one question I could answer with certainty.

"Nice to meet you, Janie," she said. "I'm Officer McHale, and this is my partner, Officer Harris. Can you tell us how old you are?"

"Fifteen."

"And do you live around here?"

I kicked the rock in front of my foot, bemused at the fact that I couldn't feel it. I couldn't feel anything. I was numb, floating in a pool of thick cotton. Everything was lesser here, less painful, less noisy, less important.

"Janie, do you live around here?" she repeated the question.

"No," I told her finally.

"I see. And where *do* you live?"

"Adamstown," I whispered, clearing my throat.

"Okay." She glanced back at her partner. "Good. Thank you. Can you tell us why you're covered in blood? Did someone hurt you?"

I began to shake my head, but froze. The nod came without thought as my father's words repeated in my head.

"Okay. We're going to get you some help, sweetheart. You're safe now. Do you know who it was that hurt you?"

"No."

"What were you doing out here in the woods at night? Why are you alone?" she asked, and there was something accusatory in her voice that I despised. I didn't mind the lying then.

"I was… With my parents. We had a cabin…" I pointed to the woods behind me.

"Okay, and where are your parents now?"

I wanted to cry, to play up the scene, but I couldn't make it happen. I kept my chin tucked into my chest instead. "Gone."

"Gone?"

"Dead," I said flatly.

The woman stayed steady, her voice unflinching. "They're dead?"

I nodded.

"And this is their blood?"

Again, I nodded.

"Okay. Can you tell me how they died?"

I started crying then, and I couldn't tell if it was real or not. "I don't know who he was. He was at the door and… I opened it, and he had a knife. He stabbed her first, my mom, and then, when my dad tried to stop him, he stabbed him, too." I was nearing hysterics, and I couldn't decide whether to be impressed with my own theatrics or concerned that I couldn't feel the real grief.

"Okay, okay…" She reached for me then, letting me fall into her arms despite my filth. Lingering in the hug felt unnatural to me, but it seemed to be what she thought was normal. My skin itched whenever I touched other people; it always had. "Shhh… it's going to be okay." When the male officer headed back our way from the car, she pulled me away from her chest, meeting my eyes for the first time. "Is the man still there? Do you know where he is? Did he follow you? How did you get away?"

"No, he's gone. I ran away," I said. "After he stabbed my dad, I just… I just ran out the door and didn't stop. I couldn't stop running."

"That was very good, Janie," she said, with a sadness in her eyes that felt real. Why should she feel sad for me, though? She didn't know me at all. "It was smart of you to run, okay? You're safe now. We're going to protect you." She pressed her lips together. "Listen, do you think you could show us where the cabin is? Where your parents are? We need to go to them. We might still be able to save them, okay? You wouldn't need to go back inside, but if you could just show us where the cabin is, if you can remember, we can try to save them and find the man who did this."

I thought about it. Honestly, the very last thing I wanted was to go back to the cabin. I never wanted to see their bodies again. But I found myself nodding, because it was what was expected of me. And, for the first time, I found myself wanting to please someone out of something that didn't feel like fear. She was eating out of my hand—I had power here. Trust. "I can try."

She smiled. "Good girl, Janie. Come on. We have backup and an ambulance on its way to make sure you're okay. Let's get in the car where it's warm, what do you say?" She stood next to me, her hand outstretched. I slid my hand inside of hers, ignoring the cringe I felt coming on instinctually, and let her lead me to the car.

To safety.

Once inside the car, I pressed my fingers together over and over, feeling the dried blood making them stick together as one thought ran through my head: *I will never let myself feel afraid again.*

CHAPTER TWENTY-FOUR

Janie

When we arrived back at the cabin, I was filled with dread. The officer rode in the back with me, her hand locked with mine. "This is it?" she asked again, as if I could somehow get it wrong.

I watched her meet the eyes of her partner in the rearview mirror. "Good thing we called for extra backup," she said quietly. There was something chilling in her tone that hadn't been there before.

"What's wrong?" I squeaked, wondering if I'd slipped up or done something wrong.

"Nothing," she assured me, too quickly. She put her other hand over mine. "We want you to stay right here, okay? Don't leave the car no matter what you see or hear. You'll be safe in here." She nodded at me, waiting for me to mimic the motion. I did, and she slid from the seat and out the door her partner held open.

I watched them round the car, their weapons drawn as they approached the door I'd left open. I wondered what they'd find. The knife would have my fingerprints on it—how would I explain that away? Perhaps I could say it was a kitchen knife, but I'd already told her he came in with a knife. Maybe I could tell her I pulled it out of my parents' bodies, but I'd already told her I ran.

As I sat in pure torment, I realized I'd need to run again. Otherwise, they'd catch me. I put my hand on the handle and pulled, shocked when the door didn't open. I pulled at it wildly, violently.

No. No. No. No.

I was stuck. Trapped.

I'd walked into my own prison sentence. I should've just kept quiet.

I saw lights flashing on my windows and looked over my shoulder, watching as two more police cars pulled into the driveway. Two sets of officers emerged; their weapons drawn. It seemed to happen in slow motion. They ran past the car where I sat, completely unnoticeable. I was as invisible as ever. But as I followed them with my gaze, I watched the officer I liked, the woman, exit the cabin. She met them on the porch. She was shaking her head. I saw the weapons drop.

They were dead; she had to be telling them.

No one else was there.

When the ambulance arrived, the officer approached my window. She opened the door cautiously.

"Come on." She wiggled her finger at me. I tried to read her face, to determine if she was angry with me, but I couldn't tell. "The EMTs are here to check you out and make sure you're okay." I took her outstretched hand, and she led me across the gravel to the ambulance. "This is Janie," she told the two women dressed in EMT uniforms. "She's had a bit of a rough night. We just need an overall wellness check."

The first one to speak had dark hair that she tucked behind her ears. "Hi, Janie. I'm Bethany. We're going to make sure you're okay, all right? Are you hurt anywhere that you know of?"

And so, the check began. I was placed on a bed inside the ambulance, where they bandaged my feet and checked my breathing and cleaned the wound on my stomach. They tossed around words that I'd heard of but didn't completely understand, like 'hypothermia' and 'malnourished,' and the all-too-familiar word, 'abuse.'

They worked in unison as my eyes began to close, the idea of sleep so intoxicating I could think of nothing else.

"We need you to stay awake for us, okay, Janie?" the one that wasn't Bethany said, rubbing her hand across my cheeks. "Just for a while longer."

I nodded.

"You're very lucky you made it out alive," she said.

Bethany tossed her a strange look, and I was instantly curious what she meant. Before I could ask, the police were back outside, talking amongst themselves. The woman officer climbed into the ambulance. "How's she doing?"

"All in all, she'll be okay. She needs some fluids and IV antibiotics for an infected wound that a doctor will probably want to stitch up, but she's going to be okay," Bethany said.

"Did you find the man?" I asked, playing along with my charade.

The officer looked at me, her expression grim. "I'm afraid not, Janie. The only person inside was a woman. Your father, the man who attacked your parents, and the murder weapon are all gone. We're organizing a search of the woods. It's possible your father went looking for you. He could still be alive." She smiled at me, and her words were meant to be reassuring, but I felt only ice in my veins.

"Do you think it was the same guy?" Bethany asked, her voice low, but not low enough I couldn't hear her.

"What do you mean? What guy?" I asked.

The officer looked at Bethany, then at me. Her chest heaved with a sharp breath. It was obvious she didn't want to say any more. "There was… a murder here before, Janie. And we never caught the man responsible. We believe," she looked at Bethany, then back at me again, "that this may have been the same man. Different MO, but we can't overlook the location. The sheriff will weigh in more when he gets here. In the meantime, can you guys get her to the hospital? We have a Perry County ambulance headed this way to transport the"—she lowered her voice again, her eyes flicking toward me sympathetically—"body."

"Sure thing," Bethany said.

Not-Bethany climbed out of the ambulance, and Bethany took a seat beside me as the officer departed the vehicle as well, waving to me gently. "They'll take care of you, sweetheart. And I'll do everything I can to find your father and the man who did this to you."

I nodded, keeping my face expressionless. As the doors closed and the engine revved, I ran over what I'd learned in my head.

"So," I asked Bethany, "there was really an attack here? Before now? Someone died?"

She appeared conflicted but eventually nodded. "About two years ago, a woman was found dead here. It was big news around town for a while, but they never found the person responsible."

"Do they think it was a serial killer?"

She offered a small smile. "Truth be told, there were so many rumors back then, I don't know what the working theory is now. In a small town like this, we don't see many deaths, not murders anyway, so it was big news. Everyone in the county had some idea about what could've happened."

"Do you think it was the same guy this time?"

"I probably shouldn't say this, but I don't believe in coincidences this big."

"They'll find him, right?" I held my breath as I asked.

She seemed uneasy. "I'm sure they'll do everything they can."

"Didn't they do that last time?"

She expelled a sad sigh. "You should probably just relax. Let me finish cleaning this wound." With that, she set to work, and I rested my head on the pillow. She hadn't answered me directly, but I considered it answer enough.

Dad hadn't been lying about the woman who'd died before, which was a lucky break on my account. Now I just had to count on the fact that the police wouldn't be able to find any trace of the murderer once again.

And that wherever my dad was, I'd done enough damage to ensure he died before they found him.

Otherwise, he'd never give up looking for me.

It would only be a matter of time before he found me again.

CHAPTER TWENTY-FIVE

Janie

While I was at the hospital getting checked out, they saw the number of improperly healed bones, bruises, and scars I had, and they asked me about my home life. I didn't know what would happen if my dad was found alive, but I knew this was my one chance to save myself. This time, I'd do it by telling the truth.

I told them everything, every single thing that Dad had ever done to Mom or me. I laid it out because I wanted to be hidden from him.

They ended up searching for him for months, looking for a body or otherwise, but nothing came up. They never found my father's body, nor any sign that he was still alive. I was placed into foster care upon my release from the hospital, where I bounced around from foster home to foster home, some great, some not so great. Each one better than the home I'd known my whole life. On my eighteenth birthday, I aged out. The family I'd been living with baked me a cake, gave me a gift card, and sent me on my way. They were kind, but they didn't love me. No one wanted teenagers.

That same day, I went to the courthouse and filed papers to have my name changed from Janie Foreman to Grace Duncan, choosing the last name of the author who had helped me through so much as a teenager.

I tried to forget about all that had happened, all that I had been through. I went to college, met my best friend, Mariah, and tried to move on. We got our first apartment together after graduation and fell in love with our jobs at the bookstore. I was happy. For the first time in my life, I was actually happy. And admitting it aloud didn't mean it would get taken away.

At least, that was what I thought.

When I'd grown comfortable in my happiness for too long, Mariah died. And everything I'd gone through was brought back up. All the pain I'd tried to ignore was suddenly front and center. I vowed to exact my revenge on the man who took her from me, just like I'd exacted my revenge on my father all those years ago.

I'd tracked Ryan down, the man who had killed my closest friend. Years before we ever spoke to each other, I spent hours watching him, searching for proof of what he'd done. But I never found it, and when I'd finally met him, he'd been different than I expected.

He was intense. So dead-set on becoming my friend, on getting to know me. He didn't have a lot of friends because of his compulsive nature. When he met someone he cared about, he dove headfirst into the relationship—platonic or otherwise. For the first time in my life, I had someone who thought I was interesting. Funny. Beautiful.

Everything my father had spent his life telling me I wasn't, Ryan swore I was. I'll admit, I got swept up in it for a minute. *I'm only human.* I was all he had, and he was all I had, and there was something magical about that. For a while, I soaked up every ounce of his attention.

We were just friends at first, but he quickly realized how damaged I was. I think his damage recognized something familiar in mine, and he clung to it for dear life. Maybe he was trying to fix himself by fixing me. Maybe he just wanted to prove that he was worthy of the love his parents had for each other.

Either way, when he asked me to marry him, I realized how far I'd taken things. I'd met him determined to bring justice to my friend, and now, not only had I not done that, but I'd let the man fall in love with me instead.

Maybe I'd fallen for him a little bit, too. After that, I toed the line of falling in love with him and planning to murder him on a daily basis. Two months of trying to decide which was more important to me as we planned our wedding.

I don't know why I said yes in the first place. Maybe some part of me wanted to explore the idea of normalcy. Wanted to know that it could happen. Wanted to know that I could be normal.

But when he'd brought up children, and I could never explain to him why I couldn't have children with him—why I'd be the worst possible parent in the world—I knew it was time. I knew I had to complete the plan I'd set into motion the day Mariah's life had been stolen.

Men needed to pay for their actions.

I couldn't let them keep getting away with hurting women, and I never would again.

He'd claimed he'd been getting sober, but I'd watched him slip back into drinking. My friend's life meant more than that. I had to make sure that was clear.

So, I'd done the only thing I could think of: I'd given Everleigh the link to the old, familiar cabin and asked her to get it to Ryan when he started talking about a honeymoon. She had no idea who Ryan really was, of course, but I knew a friendly suggestion from her on our destination would go a long way. Ryan only wanted to make me happy, after all.

And, the plan had worked. Truth be told, I had no idea the cabin was still being rented out. For years, I'd been too afraid to search for it. But, when I'd finally gotten the nerve, I was horrified by what the owner had turned it into.

He was capitalizing on our pain. The cabin had become a destination for dark tourists, like the sheriff had confirmed. A place where people could come and laugh about whether my mother's ghost, and the ghost of the other victim, still roamed. A place where they'd wonder if the serial killer who'd taken those two lives was still on the loose. Still waiting for his next victim.

That's when the idea had come to me.

The cabin, for me, was a place of loss. But also a place of rebirth. It was in this house that Grace Duncan had been born. That I'd fought for better circumstances for myself. And going back was a way of reminding myself the girl who fought back that night still existed.

Ryan had to pay for what he'd done, and he'd do so in the exact same place where my father had.

The serial killer would complete his legacy.

The plan wasn't simple. I had to think through every step—every possible avenue. Unlike the last time, I was able to plan this out, and I wanted to be prepared for anything.

Because I was tied to Ryan, I didn't want to do anything that might incriminate myself. I'd started off by locking the door with us outside the first night we were there, just to get him a bit off his game. After he'd fallen asleep, I'd gotten up and taken the screwdriver from the place beside the hot tub where I'd hidden it while Ryan was in the restroom. I used it to remove the doorknob, unlocked the door and placed the screwdriver back in the drawer after I reinstalled it. It was why I'd known exactly where the screwdriver was when we needed it next.

Then, the next morning, it was all too simple to pretend it had just been the wine we'd consumed that made us sloppy enough to think the door was locked. He knew all about being a sloppy drunk, after all.

As the plot began to form in my mind, I realized I needed to draw attention to the fact that we were being targeted. That we were scared. I wanted to do something that would make us have to go to the police for help, but I couldn't decide what.

At least, I couldn't until the day of the hike. When I saw my father, it shook me to my core. I'd always assumed he was still alive, still out there somewhere, but I never believed he would've stayed so close to the cabin. I didn't want to believe it was him, but I'd know those eyes anywhere.

He'd aged terribly. He was sickly thin where he was once all brawn. His body was filthy, wrinkled, and haggard. Time had not been kind to him.

Staring into the face of my abuser, my traumatizer, was enough to rattle me like I hadn't been in years. All at once, I was back to being a scared fifteen-year-old girl again.

It was when I saw him, once I'd regained a bit of my composure, that I knew the plan had to change. He hadn't paid enough for what he'd done, not completely, and I was going to make sure he did.

When I saw him outside of the cabin later that day and realized he'd followed us, it confirmed that he recognized me. That it was kill or be killed. It was the biggest wrench in my plan. Try as I might to keep my distance, he'd still known it was me. Though I'd changed my name and bleached my hair, something in him recognized something in me.

I wondered if he'd been living out there all those years, terrified to come out in case I'd told the police the truth about him. Surely, he must've believed the police would be looking for him. It gave me a sick pleasure to known he'd spent two decades living in the woods, cold and alone, living off scraps and bathing in the stream. There was no way to know that was what had happened for sure, I knew, and now I guessed I never would. I liked to think that was the case, anyway, that his life had been nothing but suffering. Same as mine had been before I'd escaped. Same as Mom's had been until she died.

He was there outside the cabin door that night when I'd heard the scratching and the breathing. I'd been nearly positive, but when we'd opened the door and saw the book he'd taken from me that night, the one shoved in his back pocket, I knew for sure.

The message inside was for Ryan. *Janie's dead. You're next.*

He was warning him, not realizing Ryan had no idea who Janie was, and I had no plans to tell him.

Regardless, it was the warning I needed. I knew he was coming for me then. For us. And I'd have to fight to the death.

That was fine by me. I'd made myself a promise to never be afraid again after that night so many years ago, and I'd clung to it.

Fear wasn't something I let in anymore, not really, not to my core.

The next morning, the plan became clear for me. I took the rock, painted it, and smashed our windshield. I'd half expected to have to pretend to be in the kitchen making coffee when Ryan heard it, but he was such a sound sleeper, it took me nudging him to get him awake once I was back in bed.

He was scared, but not enough to go to the police. I had to push. I was rarely a pusher where Ryan was concerned. I'd made him believe I was weak, that I needed to be taken care of, so my push went far, I believe. Carried weight, as they say.

But then the day came when my dad had slashed our tires, the day he'd come inside the cabin. He'd come for me, but my plan wasn't finished. If I killed him or let him kill me, the vacation would be over, and I wasn't finished with all I wanted to do to Ryan yet. My husband hadn't gotten the punishment he deserved.

It was fun for me to watch them go hand to hand in combat, fun to watch Ryan scare my dad off. I'd never seen that before—worry in Dad's eyes, him retreating. The many, many times I'd seen him standing over me, kicking or strangling me when I'd done something he deemed bad, had shown me many ranges of one emotion in that face—anger, rage, fury. But never fear. It was quite delightful.

To this day, I have no idea how he got inside. Did he sneak in through the door like Ryan thought? Had he found another way inside? I didn't know. Wouldn't now, anyway. It would be another mystery I'd never know the answer to.

But the slashed tires made it clear he wasn't done with me either. All the better.

He played right into my hand, if we were being honest, as I struggled to figure out how leaving would work with the timeline I had set in my mind. I needed to kill Ryan before we left the cabin, or the plan would fall apart. My father helped with that without realizing it.

I hid our phones in my bag to make sure Ryan didn't call the police. I knew he'd try, and I couldn't risk it. I didn't need them interfering just yet. It had nothing to do with them. This was between me and my husband and my father—the two men who had hurt me most in the world.

The phone calls were genius on Dad's end, though I was surprised to know he had a phone in the first place. Seeing the way he was living, I had no idea how he'd managed to charge it. But I knew his voice—the menacing way he breathed. When I was a little girl, just the sound outside my bedroom door was enough to send me into a panic attack. Now, though, it didn't faze me. Never would again.

He had no power over me anymore.

And, once I'd made them both pay for their crimes, I'd make sure no one ever thought they had power over me again.

So, when he entered the house again, I knew it was time. I'd slammed the hammer into his head, like I'd watched him slam the knife into her. I watched the light fade from his eyes, stared at the poorly-healed scars on his neck. The ones I'd given him. They were a prelude of what was to come. A prelude of the next wounds I'd inflict—fatal wounds that would never get the chance to heal.

And then, without a shred of remorse or hesitation, still riding the high from my first kill, I swung the knife at my husband's back over and over again and gave my friend the justice she deserved.

PART THREE

CHAPTER TWENTY-SIX

Grace

When it was done, I stood above the bodies with a strange sense of calm. I breathed in deep and let it out slowly. It was done. Over. They were dead, and I'd survived.

Again.

They'd done horrible things, and I had made them pay. I stepped over my husband's body, the heel of my shoe in the blood on the floor, and made my way across the room. I walked back into the closet, plugging in the phone line I'd managed to pull out while Ryan was searching for something on the shelves of cleaners.

I took a deep breath and cleared my throat. Then, with a completely steady hand, I dialed 911. I prepared myself, and in my best impression of being afraid, from the distant memories I had of such an emotion—memories that had carried me through the past few days enough that my husband believed them—I cried out for help.

"You have to help me!" I begged.

And so they did. The woman spoke to me calmly. She took my address. Asked me to describe what had happened and if I was in any danger then. I stared at my fingernails, picking the dried blood from underneath them as I relayed the murders, the fact that this man—my father, though they wouldn't know that—had come in and attacked my husband, and that with his last breath, my husband had ended the man's life to save mine.

It was all very heroic.

We stayed on the phone until the police arrived, Sheriff Ritter bringing up the rear. He looked stunned when he saw me, his eyes filled with grief. They ushered me out of the room, out of the cabin, and I was instructed to wait on the porch with the deputy, a man I recognized as one of the officers who'd worked my parents' case twenty years ago.

He watched me carefully, studying my face with an unsettling determination. "You look so familiar," he said to me at one point.

I looked at him, my face set as I dared him to say where he knew me from.

"My husband and I have been into town a few times. You may have seen me around."

He nodded slowly. If he did remember where he knew me from, I'd have a story ready to explain away any suspicions, but I didn't see that being the case. As with my father, time hadn't been kind to me. I didn't look like the little girl they'd have pictures of in the file. They hadn't taken my fingerprints. My name was different now.

There was no reason for them to find out who I was or what I'd done. And what I'd done was bring justice to a world previously unjust. Sometimes, we just owe it to ourselves.

"Do you have someone you can call? Someone who can be with you?"

I nodded. "My best friend, Everleigh. But I don't have any service here. I'll… wait until I get into town, if that's okay."

"Of course," he said quickly. "I'm sure we can arrange to get you transported back to town soon. We've already called for a tow truck for your vehicle."

"Thank you."

He stood, shoving his hands into his pockets. "You were incredibly lucky to survive something like this."

"My husband and I were told about the… well, the murders that have happened here. Was this the same?"

He seemed conflicted. "I shouldn't say too much until we know more."

"Of course." I hung my head.

"But," he said quickly, his tone forcefully light, "at least this time we caught the person responsible. Your husband made sure he can never hurt anyone again. He died a hero, ma'am."

I pressed my lips together, pretending to wipe my eyes as I kept my gaze locked with the ground. "Thank you."

"Your husband will get justice. We'll make sure of that."

"Thank you, Officer," I repeated. What did this guy want—a medal? They hadn't done anything. It was me who had brought both killers to justice, not them. They hadn't done anything for the first woman, and they hadn't done anything for my mother. It was I who'd brought justice to at least one of them, if not both. I, too, who had brought justice to Mariah. If anyone deserved thanks, it was me. But, of course, I couldn't say that.

Interrupting my thoughts, I heard the shuffle of footsteps headed our direction, and I turned my head to see Sheriff Ritter hurrying toward me. "Mrs. Graham?"

I'd never changed my last name after Ryan and I got married, but I was used to people thinking I had. I'd chosen my last name specifically, and no one would ever make me change it.

"Yes?"

"Come with me," he said, a smile growing on his face.

"What is it?" I asked, not budging.

"It's your husband, ma'am."

"What about him?" I asked, but I knew. I knew by the smile on his face and the sinking feeling in my stomach.

He nodded at me just as I heard an officer inside the cabin begin to talk. "The pulse is faint, but it's there."

I swallowed. *No.*

"Well, ma'am, he's alive."

CHAPTER TWENTY-SEVEN

Ryan

One Day Later

Bright lights shone in my eyes, my vision a sea of white and black ripples.

Dark.

Light.

Dark.

Light.

Dark.

I tried to close them, but they were held open by something I could not see.

Pain.

It was everywhere and nowhere all at once. I couldn't pinpoint where it was coming from, and yet, at the same time, it seemed to radiate from every inch of my body.

Someone, somewhere was talking.

"Ryan?" I heard, and though nothing else made sense, somehow I knew that was my name. *Ryan. I am Ryan.*

My eyelid was released, and I stumbled back into the darkness.

Down.

Down.

Down.

Beep.

Beep.

Beep.

CHAPTER TWENTY-EIGHT

Ryan

Two Days Later

There was a steady beep in the distance, drawing me from sleep like a siren's call.

Beep.

Beep.

Beep.

Beep.

My eyes were heavy, my thoughts thick and clumsy like I was trying to peel myself out of a dense fog.

Where am I?

What happened?

I didn't remember.

I didn't remember anything at all.

"Ryan? Are you awake?" I heard the beeping speed up, and a cool palm slid into mine. I opened my eyes, and it felt as if I were prying open the trunk of a car to get them to stay open. It took every ounce of my strength, but they were open, and I was staring ahead at a room I didn't recognize. "Ryan, can you hear me?" There was something—someone—to my left. A blurry figure that I couldn't bring myself to focus on.

I heard her voice.

I felt her hand in mine.

She was my wife, but I didn't know her name.

"It's me. It's… it's Grace." She was crying. My wife. The woman by my bedside. She was crying… but over what?

"Can you blink if you can hear me?"

I blinked.

At least, I think I did.

I saw the blob that was her mouth widen into a smile. She squeezed my hand. "Good! Good. Okay, how about this: blink once if you're in pain, twice if you're not."

I considered the question.

"Ryan?" she pushed. "Baby, can you hear me?"

I blinked once more.

"Are you in pain?"

Again, I blinked.

"I'll call the nurses and see if they can give you something for that." She was stroking my arm gently. "Do you remember what happened? Once for yes."

I blinked twice.

She took a deep breath, not speaking for a moment, and I found myself dipping back into the darkness.

"The man from the woods, Ryan… Do you remember him?" I was pulled back from the darkness, the room spinning lazily.

I didn't know what she was talking about. *What man?* Two blinks.

"There was a man who we met in the woods. He'd been tormenting us, he threw a rock into our windshield, stole our phones, broke into our cabin… You don't remember him? You were… Ryan, you were so kind to him. You gave him money, food, supplies… And he repaid you by trying to kill us." She leaned down and pressed her lips to my hand. The feeling sent warmth throughout my body. I loved her so much. She was amazing. "You fought back. You… you stopped him, sweetheart. You saved us. You saved my life."

I listened to her talking, still not completely understanding what she was saying. It didn't make sense. I was starting to get hints of my memories back. The cabin was there—foggy around the seams. I remembered the gravel of the drive, the crackle of sticks underfoot during a hike in the woods, but I couldn't have described the house if I needed to.

"It's okay. You don't need to push yourself. You lost a lot of blood… You had a heart attack. They lost you… *I* lost you. The doctors had to resuscitate you twice. But you came back to me. I knew you'd come back to me."

She was sobbing, and I wanted so desperately to console her, but I was fading into the darkness again without warning. "They think you're going to be okay now, but you just need to rest. I don't want you worrying." She rubbed a hand across my face, bringing me back again. I'd fight to stay awake forever if only to keep her from crying.

Her face was becoming clearer to me then, as my vision found its focus. "Do you understand what I'm saying?"

I blinked.

"I'm sorry we ever went to that awful place. I'm sorry you got hurt. I'm sorry he hurt you…"

Why was she apologizing? Nothing she'd said made it sound like her fault. It sounded like mine. The vacation had been my idea, hadn't it?

"We're going to be okay now, right?" she asked, squeezing my hand gently. "You can tell the police what I've told you, or, if you don't remember, you can just say that. They've promised me they'll go easy on you."

I blinked, thinking suddenly of the anxiety I was sure she had. I hadn't imagined that, had I? Her anxiety? Oh, God, what must this be doing to her? I narrowed my eyes at her, cocking my head to the side.

"What?" she asked, staring back at me. She was so incredibly beautiful. How had I gotten so lucky? And I'd almost lost her. I couldn't let that happen again. I tried to lift her hand in mine, tried to bring it to my lips, but failed instantly, dropping it back to my side as pain tore through the muscles of my back.

"It's okay," she said, raising our hands for me. I kissed her knuckles, then each individual finger.

"I… love… you," I croaked, my voice barely audible. If I had the choice, I would use it to say only those words for the rest of my life. She'd almost been taken from me, and I had to make sure that never happened again.

I felt my chest tighten at the thought, and then new memories began to surge, taking shape in my muddled mind.

She'd asked to leave. She'd wanted to go to the police.

I'd fought her every step of the way due to my own shortcomings. I wanted to seem brave. Strong. And I'd put her in danger instead.

I'd never make that mistake again. It was my job to protect her, to hell with my pride, and I'd make sure I did just that. Every day for the rest of our lives.

"I haven't told the police about what you did," she whispered, easing her head down onto my chest. "I'll always protect you, you know."

It took me a moment to realize what she was talking about, to remember the conversation about Mariah. To remember that she knew the secret I'd worked so hard to keep hidden. Why was she telling me that?

"When someone holds your secret, they can either protect you or hurt you. I'll always choose to protect you, because you did the same for me. You protected me, Ryan…" She kissed my jaw, and as she grew near, she whispered in my ear, "Don't make me regret my… *change of heart.*"

A knot formed in my stomach at the icy tone of her voice, and suddenly, new memories flooded my mind. They pounded into my consciousness, making me breathless as they took shape. Missing phones and library books and wine glasses and broken windshields and her skin against mine in a hot tub and locked doors and fear and pain and slashed tires and blood and… then I remembered everything.

I knew what she was saying.

What she was offering me.

I knew why she'd almost killed me.

I needed to be punished for what I'd done, and now I had been. I deserved it. She'd shown me that actions have consequences. It didn't make me love my wife any less. If anything, it made me even crazier about her. She'd held her own, fought for her friend. She'd made me realize how easy it would be to lose her and just how loyal she was to stay with me after everything I'd done.

I breathed in her scent, wanting to drown in it. Wanting to soak up every ounce of her.

Maybe it was crazy, but I'd never felt safer around her. Never felt happier. I lifted my head, pressing my lips to hers, pushing my tongue further into her mouth. I burned with desire for her in a way I never had before. It was feral, white-hot passion, blazing at my core.

The passion, which had never been lacking in the first place, was there ten-fold now.

If she could forgive me, I could forgive her.

And in that moment, just like that, with a blink of my eyes as she pulled away—a yes in the language we'd created—I did.

I forgave her and chose to love her because we were perfect for each other. If this hadn't proved that, I wasn't sure what would. The messed-up parts of me clung to the messed-up parts of her, and I'd never stop fighting to keep her with me. Keep her loving me.

We were meant to be. Destined. Fated.

I lifted my hand despite the pain, or perhaps because of it. Who didn't enjoy a little pain every now and again? It is what reminds us we are alive, after all. I cupped her waist as she leaned further into me and ran her hand along the bandage on my side just under my ribs.

The place where she'd stabbed me. I winced.

Without warning, she pushed harder into it, sending lightning-sharp pain throughout my body. Her eyes lit up with pleasure. I jolted, locking my jaw, but never breaking eye contact with her. When she released it, she smiled.

So, she was going to keep me on my toes. Keep reminding me of the power she had over me. *Bring it on.*

I welcomed the challenge, welcomed the pain of loving her and the reminder of all we'd sacrificed to be together. For the first time, I felt like I was 'seeing' her. The real her. And I loved every version of her just the same. I welcomed getting to know this side of my wife. Nothing she could ever do would make me betray her or love her any less.

A strange thought hit me as I drifted back to sleep. *I'll just have to make sure to hide the knives.*

CHAPTER TWENTY-NINE

Grace

Six Months Later

I hung my bag on the coat rack next to the door and kicked off my shoes, making my way across the living room and into the kitchen. Ryan should've been there, but the room was completely silent.

I lifted my nose in the air a bit, inhaling deeply. The house didn't smell of dinner. Why hadn't he started cooking yet? When he'd told me he wanted us to stay in and have a special night at home, I'd pictured pasta, wine, and retiring early for a long night in bed. This felt different. There was something in the air that I couldn't quite put my finger on.

I tugged open the drawer where the knives rested, shocked to see they were missing. My throat tightened. *Where are all the knives?*

"Ryan?" I called quietly, looking behind me. Vulnerability swept over me as the fear crept in.

I tried to convince myself that I wasn't in danger. I couldn't be. My dad's body had been buried. He hadn't escaped. He couldn't have come back for me. So, what then? Why was the air heavy with trepidation?

Taking quiet steps, I made my way out of the kitchen and down the hall. I didn't bother flipping on the light, choosing to move through the darkened house instead. It felt safer that way.

As I neared his office, spying the warm light underneath the door, I filled with a mix of relief and worry. Had he just ended up working late? Was that why he hadn't started dinner? Had he lost track of time? Was I overreacting and worrying for no reason? After all we'd been through, could you blame me?

I placed one hand on my stomach, trying to steady my nerves, and the other on the door handle, turning it slowly.

"Ryan?" I asked, spying him sitting at the desk as the door eased open. "What are you doing?"

He hesitated, then spun around to face me, an odd expression on his face. "I didn't hear you come in," he said simply.

"I thought you'd be cooking dinner already." Relief mixed with confusion inside my mind. Why was he staring at me like that? What was going on?

"Oh, right. Actually, I wanted to talk to you first," he said, keeping his expression unreadable.

I offered a nervous chuckle. "Okay…" Something wasn't right, but I couldn't quite put my finger on it.

He opened the top drawer of his desk and tossed out the small, yellow clam-shaped case, a pill box. It took me a moment to process what it was, but once I had, I felt indignation rising in my chest. Had he been going through my things? "Why do you have that?"

"I took it from your dresser drawer this morning," he said simply. "I think it's about time you stopped taking them."

A wave of shock washed over me. I tried quickly to decide which direction to take the conversation, to take control. *How did he find my birth control?*

Though we'd had the conversation about waiting, it felt like a lifetime ago. Instead, we'd agreed on alternate prevention methods and I'd promised him not to restart taking the pills. He didn't want them to interrupt my cycle. I'd lied, of course, but he had no right to go through my things to prove that. I'd let him live, after all.

We'd made our peace. I hadn't brought up Mariah since that night at the cabin, and he'd never brought up what happened there. We had a silent agreement… or so I thought.

"I told you I already stopped taking them," I said angrily. "Where is any of this coming from? Why are you going through my things?" I felt my blood pressure rising, my ears growing hot.

"You did tell me that," he said matter-of-factly. "And you lied. But it's time for you to stop. Lying *and* taking the pills. I want a baby, Grace. Before we're too old."

I sank down in the chair in front of him, my shoulders heavy with the weight of what he was telling me. How did he know I'd been lying? Why did he think he could tell me what I should be doing? "I don't understand where any of this is coming from. We've agreed this isn't the right time for a baby. Whether or not I'm taking the pills, frankly, isn't your concern. I thought we had an understanding…"

He was still.

"Ryan…" I prompted him. The silence was deafening, my husband's smirk filled with an air of superiority that I couldn't quite grasp. Something was happening, and I didn't like not understanding what it was.

He cocked his head to one side slightly, breaking the silence. "You know, I used to not ask any questions. I trusted you completely. Even after what you did in the cabin."

I sucked in a sharp breath. This was the first time he'd mentioned it, the only time he'd ever confirmed that he remembered my actions. I wasn't foolish enough to think that he didn't, but I believed he'd never be brave enough to mention it. I hoped he was just grateful that I'd changed my mind about him. I thought I still held the power.

"But something was bothering me," he went on. "See, you blamed me for never telling you the truth about Mariah, but you haven't told me the truth about everything either, Grace."

My heart rate accelerated. What did he mean? "Of course, I have."

"Not about these." He pushed the pills further toward me.

Relief. "Okay, yes. Fine. Not about those. But I told you I wasn't ready at the cabin. I just need more time. You can't keep pushing me on this."

He folded his hands in front of him. "No. I don't think you're going to get more time."

I sucked in a breath, jerking my head back as if I'd been slapped. "Excuse me?" Who was this man? What did he know? Whatever it was, I knew it wasn't good. The way he was looking at me was strange… menacing, even. I knew the look of danger well; I'd just never seen that look coming from him.

"We're going to have a baby *now,* Grace," he said firmly.

"What are you talking about? Where is this coming from, *Ryan?*" I tossed his name back to him. "You can't tell me what I'm going to do with my body. You can't force me to have a baby, now or ever."

His smile never wavered. In fact, he only appeared slightly more amused as he scratched his chin casually, then wagged a finger at me. "See, I think that's where you're wrong." He reached for my hand, and I let him take it because I was frozen, waiting for the other shoe to drop.

He ran a finger across mine, then withdrew his hand and opened the top drawer again. This time, he produced a single, silver key, holding it up and examining it slowly.

"What's that?" I demanded, staring at it in horror. I didn't recognize it, but I did recognize the paralyzing terror welling in my gut, taking hold of my organs. *I am in danger.* After a lifetime of escaping it, I'd walked right into his office that night, blissfully unaware of the danger that was waiting. But now, I knew. I knew before he spoke the words.

He didn't answer. Instead, he said, "I love you, Grace. More than life. More than anything in this world. I'd do anything for you.

But, sometimes, things between us just don't feel even. Because you have *so* many more secrets than me. At least, you did. I only have one more, and then, once I've told you, we're going to spill all of yours."

"What are you talking about?" I asked, my voice powerless as I felt chills creeping along my skin. He wasn't lying. I could see it in his eyes. *What does he know? What has he done?*

"I saw you that night, too."

I froze, my throat tight as I struggled to understand.

He narrowed his gaze at me, leaning forward slightly. "I saw you the night I hit Mariah. That's my final secret. Meeting you wasn't an accident, and it wasn't all because you'd looked for me. I'd looked for you, too. I needed to keep you quiet. I needed to find out what you'd seen, and what you were planning to tell. I'd watched you for years before I talked to you, too."

I stared at him, unable to speak. *How is it possible? How could I not have known?*

"I've told you I would never tell anyone what happened…" I said finally.

He gave a small, slow nod. "You did. But there was a time when I didn't believe it. Before I knew you. When I spent time researching you. Except there was no *you*. It was as if you'd sprang up from the ground, fully formed. Grace Duncan, age eighteen. Before that, I couldn't find a single record of you. You told me you grew up in Raleigh, but I found nothing."

"It's a common name," I said, my brows knitting together, lies at the ready. I knew how to fumble my way through this part. "What exactly are you implying?"

He ran a finger across the key, placing it in his palm and then laying it back down. "Common enough, sure. But odd that I couldn't find you anywhere. I called the high school you claimed to have gone to, after we started dating, and they had no record of you. None."

"Th-that has to be a—"

"And none of it made any sense, but I was willing to let it go because I loved you, and I believed you loved me—"

"I *do* love you," I argued, fury beginning to override the fear. I needed to remember who I was, what I had survived. "I think you should be careful what you're implying."

"Oh, I'm not *implying* anything," he said, a carefree lilt to his tone that had me seething. "I'm telling you what I know, Grace. Or should I say… *Janie?*"

Janie. My fury washed away in an instant, leaving pure horror in its wake. My skin was ice cold at the mention of my old name. Janie felt like a stranger to me. She was not me anymore, but that didn't stop the involuntary flinch of recognition.

"What are you talking about?" I managed to squeak out.

He stared me dead in the eye, speaking slowly, his words measured.

"See, I recognized the name of the school on that library book's barcode. And then when I heard that man from the cabin say Janie, that night at the window, I remembered the message, that name, from inside. Janie's dead, you're next. *His warning, so I thought.* So, after we got home, I looked it up. I searched for anyone named Janie, relating to that school and that cabin." The conversation paused as we stared at each other, the truth resting between us. "I think you know what I found."

I blinked, unresponsive. I felt numb. Angry. Terrified. The emotions swirled through me, each fighting to take control, but I fought them down.

"I could never find anything about Grace Duncan because Grace Duncan didn't exist. Not before 2001." He clicked his tongue. "Your school was even nice enough to send me an old yearbook." One corner of his mouth upturned. "You were really a cute kid."

"What do you want?" I asked, clutching my hands in my lap. My nails dug into my palms, but I hardly noticed.

"To even the playing field," he said, picking up the key again. "See, I lied to you about Mariah, and about seeing you that night, but you lied to me about who you were, Grace, about being on birth control, and about why you killed your father."

My father. So, he knew about that, too. I sucked in a breath. For most of my life, all I'd owned were my secrets. Now, those didn't even belong to me. "That man was awful to me… You don't understand."

"I'm not saying I blame you, sweetheart." He reached for my hand once more, rubbing my fingers gently. His eyes were soft then, for the first time. There was the man I knew. The man who made me feel safe. I reveled in his loving gaze for the moment, but in an instant, he was gone again. "I know you had your reasons, just like I can understand why you felt you had to hurt me that night. But you'll understand that I needed a bit of an insurance policy to make sure you didn't do that again. It was fun, for a while, to live on edge, wondering what you were thinking… But that could only last so long. Now that we're going to have a family, I needed your assurance that you'd never hurt me again."

"What do you mean?"

He wiggled the key in between his fingers. "It's simple, really. Every piece of evidence. Every picture of you, every article I could find about what happened at the cabin, plus a letter from me explaining exactly what happened the day I was stabbed… It's all locked away safely in a safety deposit box at my parents' bank. Think of it like an insurance policy."

Dread rolled through me as I stared at him, fury seething in my stomach. "I've added my parents as payable on death, so if anything were to happen to me, they'd be the ones to get the box… and all of its contents."

My eyes darted to the key as I processed what he was saying. Now I understood why I'd felt that danger was coming. As usual, my instincts had been right. I had to stop this. "Of course, there is more than one key. Getting rid of this one would do no good," he said, reading my mind.

"What do you want?" I asked again, my jaw tight.

"I don't want anything from you, Grace. Except your love. And a family. But I wanted to be honest with you, about everything. I wanted you to understand what's at stake if you were to... ever try anything foolish again."

"And how do I know that even if I do nothing to hurt you ever again, you won't do something to implicate me anyway? Or what if something else happened to you... a car accident? Something I didn't cause. Your parents would get those papers then too, and I'd have no way to stop it. You'd be punishing me even if I was innocent. There has to be another way. Where's *my* insurance? Who's protecting me in all of this?"

He twisted his lips, running a finger across the key again. "That's why we really shouldn't wait to have a child. Of course, once we do, once our baby is here, the terms would need to be... renegotiated. This is to protect us both, you understand. I would never want our child to be without either of us."

"I don't understand why you feel like you need to do this... You'd honestly want to blackmail me into having a child with you?"

He pursed his lips, staring at me in disbelief.

"I don't consider it blackmail, Grace. Because I do love you and you love me. Let's just call it an incentive, hm? It's simple, really. I'm protecting myself from you, and you from me. A child will do that. A child will fix us. We've both been given the chance to do something unforgivable and come back from it. Neither of us need to exploit the other's goodness. I will protect your secret, just like you're protecting mine. And we will raise our family and build something better than either of us had. Because I love you. And because *you* love *me*."

He picked up the case of pills. "So, what do you say?"

I nodded stiffly, not meeting his eyes. No matter what he called it, it was blackmail. I'd underestimated him, to my own detriment. I'd let myself believe that he could love me. That he could want me to be happy. I'd punished him and, in turn, punished myself.

"Toss them out," I muttered finally.

"Attagirl," he said slyly, wasting no time tossing the pills into the trash before clapping his hands together. He stood from the desk and walked toward me, but I stayed still.

His face fell. "Don't be afraid of me."

"I'm not," I said softly, and I wasn't. Now that I understood what was happening, had a firm grasp on my new reality, the fear I'd felt moments ago had disappeared. I'd known true fear living with my father, and this wasn't that. Ryan did love me, more than I'd ever been loved before, even if it was in his own twisted, sick way. The same way I loved him. Despite our flaws. Despite the way the hatred intertwined with love most days. I was still angry, of course. That wouldn't fade so quickly. I'd still look for a way out of this, but I wasn't afraid anymore. I wasn't in danger as long as I followed his rules. He'd followed mine long enough, it wouldn't hurt to let him think he'd gained the upper hand while I found my footing once again.

Nothing about our marriage was conventional, but I didn't expect it to be.

I stepped forward, bitterness rising in my chest as I fell into his arms. His was the only touch that didn't make my skin crawl. He lowered his lips to my ear.

"I love you," he said.

"I love you, too." It wasn't a lie.

"We're going to be okay now. You know that, right?"

I nodded against his chest. I did know. Somehow, I knew. Neither of us had any choice. He was right, I hadn't ruled out trying to kill him again down the road, but this plan would certainly make things harder.

Well played, dear husband.

If he stayed on his best behavior, letting him live made the most sense. It was just easier. Perhaps he was thinking the same thing about me. Letting me keep my secret just made life easier for him.

"'When someone holds your secret, they can either protect you or hurt you.' Those are your words. For so long, you've held my secrets, but now, I hold yours too, Grace. We're equals. And I will always protect you."

I lifted my head to look at him, pressing my lips to his gently. So, he still worshipped me, still wanted to protect me, but now he knew my secrets. I had no idea what I was going to do with that information, but as I snaked my hand into his back pocket, my tongue into his mouth, I knew I was going to have a hell of a lot of fun figuring it out.

Death has a smell, one I could recall, and probably would be able to for the rest of my life. It has a feeling, too. *Witnessing* death has a feeling, I mean. It's hard to explain if you haven't experienced it. Electricity pulses through your veins, creeping to every corner of your body as if their energy has passed from them to you with their last breath.

Your chest swells with something hot and exhilarating. Freedom envelops you. I'd never felt that jittery feeling outside of the moments I'd looked death in the face—first the baby's, then my mother's, and finally my father's.

But as I kissed my husband harder, feeling his hands wrap around my waist, our hearts beating in unison, just thin fabric, bones and skin separating them, I discovered happiness has a feeling, too. I guessed it was the first time I'd allowed myself to feel it, really feel it, in so long.

As it turned out, I liked both feelings equally.

In fact, they felt almost identical.

I could work with that.

A LETTER FROM KIERSTEN

Dear Reader,

Thank you so much for choosing to read *Just Married*. If you enjoyed this twisted story, and want to keep up to date with all my latest releases, just sign up at the following link. Your email address will never be shared, and you can unsubscribe at any time.

www.bookouture.com/kiersten-modglin

A few years ago, my family and I took a trip to a peaceful mountain cabin in the Great Smoky Mountains of Tennessee. Set up just like the cabin in this story, we had an entire wall made of windows that overlooked the woods outside. While my husband found it peaceful, I found it unnerving. "What if someone's out there?" I wondered. "Watching us?"

From there, this story really began to take shape in my mind and much of it was plotted before the trip was over. (Traveling with a thriller author is loads of fun, can't you tell?) I'm pleased to say the trip was much less eventful than the events that transpired in this story, but I had so much fun creating it for you and getting to share and explore Grace and Ryan's marriage full of secrets.

I hope you loved the story that unfolded in *Just Married*, and if you did, I would be so grateful if you could write a review. Reviews truly mean the world to me as I love learning what my readers thought of my novels, and each review makes such a difference in helping new readers to discover one of my books for the first time.

I absolutely adore hearing from my readers! If you'd like to get in touch, please don't hesitate to do so. You can always find me on Instagram, Facebook, Twitter, Goodreads, TikTok, or my website. You can also send me an email here: contact@kierstenmodglinauthor.com

I can't wait to hear from you!

Thanks again for reading!
XO,
Kiersten

@kierstenmodglinauthor

@kierstenmodglinauthor

@kierstenmodglinauthor

@kmodglinauthor

kierstenmodglinauthor.com

ACKNOWLEDGMENTS

First and foremost, to my amazing husband and beautiful little girl, thank you both for believing in me every step of the way. Thank you for cheering me on, celebrating every success, and for making living with an always-on-a-deadline, sometimes cranky, usually daydreaming writer look easy. I'm so grateful to be able to spend this life with you both. We've dreamed of this day, loves. We did it!

To my friend, Emerald O'Brien, thank you for believing in this book from the moment I told you the idea. Thank you for laughing with me as I wrote with every light in the house on and for always being my biggest cheerleader.

To my immensely talented editor, Maisie Lawrence, thank you for seeing the vision I had for this story and making it a thousand times better. I'm so grateful and lucky to work with someone who truly gets my writing, asks the hard questions, and pushes me to strive for greatness, because these characters deserve nothing less. Thank you for your advice, for believing in me, rooting for me, and making my lifelong dream a reality.

To the incredible team at Bookouture, whom I consider myself insanely lucky to be able to work with, thank you for all you do! Thank you for being a champion for great stories, for your tireless efforts to connect amazing readers with novels they'll (hopefully) love, and for taking a chance on my work. I've dreamed of this day for so long and it really is better than I could've ever hoped for.

To my cover designer, Lisa Horton, thank you for putting so much effort into creating the stunning bow atop this chilling package. I'm in awe of your creativity and talent!

To my loyal readers, thank you for being excited for each new story without hesitation. Thank you for your unending support, for the emails, the social media posts, the reviews, the recommendations, and the book club invitations. I'm so thankful for every single one of you.

Last but certainly not least, to you, thank you for reading this story. There was a time, not so long ago, when I dreamed of the day when someone would read my words, meet my characters, and love the journey I was able to take them on. I wished for this moment, and for you, so for that, I'm incredibly grateful to you. Thank you for supporting my art and my dream.

Whether this is your first Kiersten Modglin novel, or your twenty-fifth, I hope it was everything you hoped for and nothing like you expected.

Lu

SEP - - 2021

June 14/23 idP

Manufactured by Amazon.ca
Bolton, ON